Love Street

Susan Perly

Love Street ~ a novel

The Porcupine's Quill

CANADIAN CATALOGUING IN PUBLICATION DATA

Perly, Susan
Love Street

ISBN 0-88984-224-8

1. Title.

PS8581.E7267L68 2001   C813'.6   C2001-930271-1
PR9199.3.P47L68 2001

Published by The Porcupine's Quill,
68 Main Street, Erin, Ontario NOB 1TO.

Excerpts from 'When The Shoe Fits' and 'Keng's Disciple'
are by Thomas Merton, from *The Way of Chuang Tzu*,
copyright © 1965 by The Abbey of Gethsemani.
Reprinted by permission of New Directions Publishing Corp.

Represented in Canada by the Literary Press Group.
Trade orders are available from General Distribution Services.

We acknowledge the support of the Ontario Arts Council,
and the Canada Council for the Arts for our publishing program.
The financial support of the Government of Canada
through the Book Publishing Industry Development Program
is also gratefully acknowledged.

1   2   3   •   03   02   01

Canada

for D.

1

:... ... would a matchbox as Sam Cooke the great Sam Cooke and would a matchbox hold my clothes – at the Harlem Square Club that Saturday night '63 ... ... and wondering which way to go?

It is Tuesday or Wednesday of that I am absolutely certain. And yesterday whichever if it was Monday or Tuesday I ran into a man who said.

The man said to me ——

—— 'I was reading the other day here this *The Way of Chuang Tzu* translated don't forget to get the one by Thomas with an h Merton.

'And there where, baby, it says,' —— this man I met at it was the corner of oy and ov, said to me, said from when that shoe, and said, and when that shoe, he said, and said, 'Don't forget,' he said.

He said, 'From there where from "When the Shoe Fits" it says and you know it's so ——, where it says, and it goes something like this:

' "Easy is right. Begin right

' "And you are easy.

' "Continue easy and you are right.

' "The right way to go easy

' "Is to forget the right way

' "And forget that the going is easy." '

The Anchorite.

Anchoress.

Hey baby. Yeah. Uh-huh. You know who I'm talking to. You and me baby. That table for two — that private wavelength you've been hoping to dial up on that radio. Sure. You wondered what's she do in them off the air hours. Baby I'm going to do a little show just for you. Spin you some of my more private platters. This is going out to you know who I'm talking about who I hope you got my message. — Say I sure hope you sure heard me there last night okay? (Was that a wasp or a love bug going into the wood?) I got my record player suitcase.

And I want to tell you something. Have you ever felt this way? (There you are sister, you're where you were going) — Where — You're *where* am I? You're where *am* I? You're How do I get to where I want to go? And then about ten years later you're, Hey I'm where I was going only I didn't know it. How come I'm the last one to know? Yeah I'm telling you about it. Okay so along that line, lines here — here's some ————— some, let's see ——— Roland Kirk. Who which we missed your birthday last week, Mr Kirk, so many happy 59s, to you from belated last Monday ... ... blew me dye yet like —— Indigo Am I Readyed Yet for Heaven Yet Yet Street like little and you know illicit type faces in a little sound suitcase come out, loud speaking licks ill suited for aught — but love. How about a little 'No Tonic Pres'? Uh-huh ...

a little Tao of the Blues.

Mr Kirk there playing with himself and his tripartite sax agreement out of heaven's junkyard something to kill us, make us sweet.

I see a big old high babies mother of a pillar out there. Some godly great big bod son of Mr and Mrs Heap out there.

Some days that Mr Kirk's got three of them fine offspring brethren breathing down pillar clouds of Heapdom down inside his throats, he's reeding, baby, he's reeding. May it rain down on us like rolandkirkische saxophones today we would be most grateful, to above. Speaking of tlie.

Did I ever tell you about the time.

Did I ever tell about the girl once I killed myself on the air where Mr Mayfield plays or we're saving that for rainy day.

And I'm going to play you a little something. A pyre which came my way. Now be good children don't ask too many questions. I'm going to lay some good spare change on some of our nicest most well-behaved peace officers might just be listing here on this particular air-waves. Don't worry brother I'm not going to tell your baby on you. So the short story's we're going to get around to which where the little bread crumb here is the lost pain of it all we'll get to later.

This is Mercy talking to you in the Ultima Thule. Remember D.J. Tootie? Remember old Eidelon of Evenfall, hisself? Remember the Old Limn-Master? Remember Daddy Dust? Remember Ready Teddy and the Theres? Remember, oh remember it all. Remember Johnny Front now that was a good one. Johnny Front, remember? I always thought of Johnny Front as Mr Front before I knew he was so sweet. He was sweet. Oh, saints alive, that man was. Saint Sweet, those times. Remember Mr W? Mr Big? Remember Doctor Daddy? Now that man had a speculum you did not want on which to on which of to you know what I'm saying here, too much get on that speculum and you'd better ride, best, rather that you'd ever want to go speculate. Remember Professor Preposition? Make that Prep a Prop and you'll be fine. Remember never mind Daddy Dust remember Daddy Mommawell? Remember Motherwell Springs? Remember Rothko Road? Remember Big Red and the Rot Net? Remember way those ink tushies used to draw you to remember the delicatenesses of the delicate's delicatessen used to go glow in the night, having dropped their nesses of neon while you essed a Reb Mingus on pastrami.

Remember how some days when it was hard to get rid of the sadness, you turned me on at night down by the river's want you were feeling water on you, we are always in the tears of things. Good morning, babies. It's so dark out.

You might have found me, – photograph, daguerreotype, – self-portrait of me and my noose – of me out there in some antique or flea, you might have been marcheing the flea baby and found that nice nudie of me, sure.

Good morning, babies. Now. And now we're back in that dark part of the morning. That darkest part, baby I hope you're with me today. I think I can feel you out there with me – and it is so dark out there today, isn't it. Sure. I know. It's the dark time of the when the species gets afraid feels afraid. You know – were feeling bad before weren't you? – about 2–2:30? About a quarter to three? About quarter after three? But you know, baby now's the real tough time. Now's the one's the hardest going to be to get through. That's right. Stick around, we're I'm not going anywhere at this end when the human species is afraid to be found awake or even in some found sleep, honey-child when this sky over the human settlement is full of the river and full of the lake. And the sky baby heaven's sitting mighty low on Miss River. Are you with me, baby? I know you're out there. You're feeling heaven right now – aren't you. I know you're out there, baby. I know you can hear the sound of my voice. And heaven's saliva don't you know is wetting down those shutters and those jalousies and the saliva of heaven is busy B & Eng your bed with its fine fettled fog girdles for dreams to dream on. And you can dream on. Dream along with Mercy here – on Love Street. Stick around whether you're try-ing to find a couple zees in the cool of the morning. Maybe you've been digging that dark night with St John of the Cross a long tonight tonight baby and you've been saying ———————————— Well just lay boy. Just like Mercy Dog bring you some platters to dream on. For those of you with

| 10

your heads down in the soup bowl – okay. Those of you with your heads up on the edge of the bowl – good for you too. And those of you stepping up there above the level of the sea – okay. Here's some Percy Mayfield for those. – Now why don't we let – here's some Percy Mayfield break and enter your heart right now. Here's Mr Mayfield. For those of you hurting out there … 'Life Is Suicide'… …

Hey you know husband number two used to say Did anybody ever tell you you sound like Barry White when you do that. Do that: Do what? Oh you know what, don't you boys. Sure you do. Well #2, L-o-o-o-o-o-v-v-e. He didn't appreciate … … Well Mr Loosey-deucey don't you just wish you that old spice back. That with her low voice. I guess there's a few gents out there passing some time with St John of the Cross who don't mind. Yeah. Now I'm going to bring you somebody who to break and enter your hearts babies – hang in – At 4 – in that – dark-part of the morning. This is Mercy. Mercy Baby. Another morning on Love Street. With Mercy on Love Street.

That air out there begging for rain. Must be 100 per cent out there now. You might find the same. Here's some Percy early yevery day yevery cycle of self-suiciding put off by lifers in for 'Life Is Suicide', liking it as the tune of a life sentence so soft and sentient we could be penitents to Saint Augustine I believe I hear out there calling us to be his heat prayer. Here's Mr Post Winter Ball all trained up into the season Percy Mayfield then here there now – for – you –

The Boogie-Woogie Anchoress of Ursulines.

Just outside – down on the radio patio under the nightshade – taking a little asthma cigarette – inhaling those skirts I just briefly before reentering the air of you touched a rolled banana leaf – it was softer than I thought.

And baby, I swear it's got that fragrance outside – in this night which is mourning —— in this morning light so night, so right for you know what I bet what – jasmine, that ginger stuff

... I bet you might have a banana leaf all nice and rolled up outside like some kind of Man now that's what I call a joint well go on and touch it. Get thee into that green nun, baby, nery, into that green skirt greenery, so sensible in the legends of the she and he essence of just essing and fressing fresh air to end soft he's curtains tits up this heat goes on any longer, dry. Oh my. Yes. Do. Yes. Yes. Go on out yonder and just gander those banana-fronds. Aren't they something? Aren't they? They make it all worthwhile. Go on. Go ahead. You can take me with you, go on. Let's bring in: well I think some Pres speaking of down in the old stritch and manzanillo manzana manzello cello chest bell and whistle graveyard of love some would, go now a little off the tonic and into the Oscar. And a little Teddy and Pres would go just dandy about now – of the Oscar and the President. Yeah. Let me lay the President, down on Peterson ... ... of —— Love. With a little 'Prisoner of Love' breaking out of that life sentence somebody do not break out this prisoner of heat, man this dry is a ball and chain the Academy of Love is waiting, Oscar, no rain at least let us tinkle them keys.

... ... All right. Happy Birthday Oscar Peterson. 70, even, today.

Clear skies, good morning Miss Lazy Bones. What're you all doing in bed yet. I hope it was a good time last night ... ... It's nice and cool this morning ... ... only 82 degrees – it's still pekinese there – Let the anchor-ess – why don't we let – now in the wee hours we could try on a little James Brown 'Try Me' – just drift off there because it's all going to be ... ... a little 'Try Me', now ... ...

... ... Off the *Live at the Apollo, 1962*, a little 'Try Me'... Did you get a good sleep?

You know I was and but now I think I'll skip ahead and get in some more of that nice in the dark hours do with some 'I Don't Mind' and you can back catch some winks more ... ...

You *are* going to miss me. Ugh! I feel so ugly this morning.

You know what I mean, people. Oh man you've been dreaming of that cute baby you see at your local coffee iv joint ain'tcha been lately – Sure, Mercy knows – maybe he's been doing the same, brother, sister that bod might want to be more than your brother to you watching you hook up that intravenous to-stay caffeine. Sure. And yesterday you wore that pretty top – The tight one, didn't ya? And wore under that pretty top those tight personal mushroom device separator nice tight jeans didn't you. With the no socks and those nice black high pumps. And where is he? He's nowhere – that's where. He's sleeping off some other dame, sleeping her off with her right there, sleeping him off – so to hell with the guy right boys – to g.h.a. zee hell with the boy. You're going slopsville this morning. You're going to wear that ugly, that awful, that pointless, that jointless oink-ing up in those habanero Scovilles of X's of extra-large baby-ment you most ugly ugly ugly ugly evaporation permission whatevers in that closet. He wants to sleep with another t'ell with the ting. Right.

And so you go out with that baggy baggy baggy baghdad baby T on with those worst most dirty khaki short-shorts which show everything – everything ugly you got to show. And just to put a little cream in the coffee he's not even there yester-day to order when boys you looked so good in your best under-shirt, and ladies you looked quite handsomely in the Miss Triple Letters of the Alphabet of sticky-outys – and I'm not going to ask if it's padded or not Boys and Girls I do not mind. Sometime I'm going to tell you a story about the three of us. Me Kleenex and my double – well Triple-A early word but never mind that for a which, children the point is man I feel ugly today. I washed my big fat wormy fritzball today and it looked like a human pancake. It looked like the pancake club for men. It looked like it needed some maple surple and got it – Man it is surely a bad rug day here down in this over dish looking up at the river I'm telling you. And don't you just know when you got in your artificial uglies with that pancake and syrup down over your ears where your waves used to be, Mr Possible's going to walk in the door, oh yes he is. Mr Possible's going to walk in the door with his good hair on this nice clean pressed shirt and his nice deck shoes with the nice no socks and he's going to turn around his morning bean caffeine ID IV device and he's going to go.

Man I thought she was Mrs Possible there but baby I must've been dreaming, I must've been out of my head, I must have been noggin on vacation, I must have been kopf gone koyach kaput baby. You know the one I told you about? I see her every morning.

I see her every morning there at the coffee joint, not long after I get out of bed. Oh yes I see her at the coffee joint – don't you, fellows? – just after I get out of bed. And I think she's a Mrs Possible, baby but now today right there are 20 minutes after eight I put my glasses on and even if they were stuck together with baling wire and masking tape and paper clips and safety pins and momma! I must have been right clear plain straight up plumb neat out of my head. Oh man I should've stood in bed. Oh man the woman was ugly. She was ugly. Oh man, baby I should've stood in bed.

Oh she was remember those baggy pants.

Oh Lord tell me about it, girl was wearing those baggy baggy baggy baggy baggy baghdad pants. And she was wearing some skeleton of the desert on top, she's wearing some Badwater cat on her back, she's wearing some dead thing on her back there, she's wearing some gone cat on her front, that woman I think is Mrs Possible, children, that boy I think is the girl for me, baby, she she's wearing a bad cat set of bones on the front there and some corpse looking for water there on the back. And ugly! Oh tell me about it ugly. Ugly, ugly, ugly, oh tell me about it, ugly.

And that's what he's thinking there, he lays his eyes on me.

That's where it was wasn't it eh there Honeys why just yesterday when you decided to go out and stir your stubs and get stir fried early in the morning, 'cause you been stirred by thoughts of him all the night. I know. And I know.

I know.

I know.

And I know you know what children – I know you're not feeling ugly now. I know you're not feeling too ugly now. I know you're not feeling too ugly at all now are you? Just a lying there in your good bed, dreaming of that dreamboat. Why you're already forgot you looked like a boat come off the mooring waking a – an – anchorette pancake that murple surple dried and kind of stringied you out there with it and your face was going solaire sensitive from those anti-living pills you got prescribed to take. You been going antibiotic lately child and now you're a buckwheat dub for antibodies with a beat when that sung surple and you know what what what care do you. I do you. You don't care. 'Cause you're not ugly. You love your maple toupee, even if it is growing out of your head. You don't care if you're baghdad inlines baby you do not care. 'Cause you been spending some hours with Mr Beautiful up in your head.

And I'm going to tell you something.

And I'm going to tell you something right now it's done.

And I'm going to tell you something right now.

And I do believe we drifted off back there getting lost off of that 'Try Me' into I feel weak myself into right into 'Lost Someone' and I'm feeling weak, one side, and I turned myself over, I felt awful weak on the other side I had to go back and 'Try Me' again just to feel so good and weak all over on both sides, again. Mr James Brown, Ladies and Gentlemen. Wake up! There's a naked lady in your room. A naked Anchoress calling you. The Naked Anchoress, in the line. Wake up! There's a lady wearing radio clothes for the blind, time to wake up. It's still a little lap hot dog yet we're going to be pit bull later. By high noon baby it'll be eat your face off so take care. All cost now you stay away from that sunny of the street. You're getting too in the mood, well, how's about some St James now. Yeah you know it before I did. St James Booker . . . . . .

That was some 'Black Night'. Made me think about the good things. Remember *Last Tango in Paris?* Don't you love those weak love oranges? Now that was talking about camera work worthy of being on the radio you could just close your eyes and listen to that camera swing. Before that was 'On the Sunny Side of the Street'. Yeah coming to you with the Boogie-Woogie Anchoress of Ursulines. Now let's bring up some 'Streets of Fire' just for the hell of it . . . . . .

. . . . . . And Bruce wanted to talk to Sam there a bit cuddle up a bit it seemed looked like. Off the *Darkness at the Edge of Town*, 'Streets of Fire', then 'Feel It' from the *Sam Cooke Live at the Harlem Square Club, 1963*, Mr Sam Cooke. No but yeah we threw in a little 'Prove It All Night', just before 'Feel It'.

Oh Baby I got to tell you, all this music and all this shnarfing man baby I've had so much already this morning, I got to tell you I went through a whole pack of smokes. I'm cutting back. Used to smoke Camels. Now I'm down to the one-hump kind. Hey yeah w – what was that. Righto city, baby. That's some junkyard boys that anchor-ess has got herself there. Man these tin cans rattling around there when she inspires. To make you touch some whole lot of who all just got a breast turkey rye and boys? Honey she's got a body shop and you know what you're right. I got body parts in my body parts today, man, mother have Mercy on the air out there.

Can you hear the air pleading.

Can you hear the air begging, baby.

Can you hear the air asking Have Mercy baby please let me rain. Doesn't anybody love stormy weather out there any more
. . .

And I'm going to be spelled by heaven, in time.

Datura Tree.

You know I was sitting out in the dark just before I came in looking at the Datura. Sitting under the leaves. Drawing with my hand. Do you know how those buds when they open, on the nightshade, look, don't you, have you ever noticed like some kind of a bird with its head up into the leaf thing there call it what. And that kind of scallopy leaf.

And #2 about ten fifteen later was more dropping like that bird and thing it's sticking its head up into are one.

And then a small kind of sweep like it's all a little sense of a broom.

Which makes me want to say:

#4 a droop of a close bodice and a full curved-in crinoline.

#5 Now this crinoline is messed up and like there was wind where there is none, only desire.

Like the nightshade bloom is leaning forward and leaning back with the bottom half. Like the nightshade bloom is hanging down not bloomed yet like its own spike décolletage. White trumpets wearing high heels.

#6 A try at that close bodice and the shower crinoline coming out.

A half try, just the nip bodice.

A nip bodice again.

Like a hummer, like a
green gem, like an anonymous
green hummer, like a hummer
with no eyes, like a hummer whose
beak is the stem of the tree,
like a pod gone a hummer.

#7

Two leaf points like *Fantasia* Kirby Puckett toes.

The ends of the skirts lifted up.

One hanging down.

The sense of gathering close, like the pod skirt nightshade

bloom lifted up is close-bound Chinese feet toes curled up into it, outside.

The White Ginger by the Fountain

A dirty scribble at the top and the long leaf, the little twirl scribble. Getting the line of it.

White Ginger.

The long out stem, the long hanging green, the tall tight up top stem things, a parrot-green sense.

White Ginger.

A scribble. A prayer mountain scribble smoke thread green mountain V's, back, the green hot dog; then out front.

The White Ginger.

Tall thing creature, three hands begging, pointing, waving. No wind. Little bud off to left side.

The White Ginger.

Just that nice bloom all big inward leaves.

Good morning, children, this is your mother here. Welcome back to Rapture Alley. Momma you been hiding the good stuff on me. But Momma had her times didn't she children, oh Momma had her times around those couple-few blocks, be assured of that. Momma's been around the clock a few times well, let's. Well, let's see. Well Lordy, let's not even have again another one of these. Remember back some of you old-timers August 16 what was his name who got beaned and killed. Fighter ... ... Those principals ... And now let's see well back only some three years we never even got down with Brother Andrew yet, we still've got a full six days to Andrew's coming of back then there but Andrew's going to be knock knock knocking on La La's door, there ... ... In those calm days of the Child's anonymity, and those calm days when all season we waited to 'Can't Get Started', with you, not even an A, them hurricane days, then that green light, cast over all, and the strange love, seeing one other human down that Exchange and I did Alley love with him just as Andrew spoke in our ears such devastation; knowing you're going to die, does something to you. What if you live? After that? And now let's see now in those low elevation revelation Yellow Days graveyards are full of we ain't not yet never ever have we? Combated it yet. But as being as that may be as it is let this go on out then to Mr W … Mr W You know who you are, baby, sure you do. You and me had some good times here past times didn't we. We sure did. He's gone and left me, people, some time back but I sure do as the song says remember those good times. It was that stroke when he was but 53 which changed his eyes so. Before that? – age say he comes out with that photograph of him I took I love so, so say, say he's '55 it's going to be he's 36 in '55 and he's looking I mean: those calamus eyes. I mean I remember Mr Daddy. And I want to tell you something, children — and this recent man, this new man (but Mr Daddy I didn't desert you, not even in the desert, not even with a rabid moose jumped up and was a gold El Dorado of evenfall's ungelet eyelet shirt, this man I meet at the corner of Real and oy or was it Real and Conti, this St Conti or he looked like he was willing to make such a sacrifice play for me I could have hit him as Abraham, but) when I woke up in the morning and I said his name to myself, most intimately, it was always the other name never went and he was Abraham, and Mr W in my deepest true intimate emotion was Mr W, to me. It had been too long, knowing him by that name. Children, you know what you love already. And to me it goes, then, let me say then, without saying being as the reason being is was is that being goes without having to be — articulated as far as you're this man has X-ray eyes and they ain't even not yet yet yet have invented X-rays yet typething. Incarnation? Yeah. Re – I do not know. But I do know eyes travel in time as well as space, and this Abraham of lately, here, is some kind of Mr W eyes I can tell, you, will tell you, baby, that much. I remember, in Washington, in the District of Columbia remembering him in the perishing heat one May after the early blossoms had fallen their rain, pink, and all was sultry. There was this deep pools' sense of it all and also the smell of his beard when first I grazed it, browsing the scent of Abraham's beard which did remind me of Mr W in the days we stood up and drank coffee and talked of money and the blues which felt just right, and even then the yellow had taken many. It was hard, later, when he had that stroke, to imagine how lively his eyes had been even at 50, and even at 60 and how much Abraham did remind me of Mr W ... Mr W? By he's midfifties he looks, in photographs of him, taken at the time, as if he were in his eighties, and when he's not even 68 he looks like the 176 he turns last May. Everybody knows where they are going – we just do not right there, baby, there on your pillow know there yet the yet here there of the circumstances of it yet – what proportion of our life will be — prepositional claws and which and which will be sweet verbal use. I remember when he used to love me when he was but a young man of before the stroke. At 48 he looked barely 40, at 54 he looked 95. It was in the eyes. Not sad. Gone. Some other kind of music was playing, some other kind of wartime. Like a war observer so keen his eyes were sex gone to shellshock watery. I loved the man. I've always had a soft spot for journalists. I have loved more than one man from Brooklyn. I have had occasion to do things, in Philly. Oh and not even 60 he was a man with a long white beard and a long white wide beard and these lost eyes of nowhere. Gone. But in the beginning his eyes had everything, every place. I used to like to look at his eyes move. He was a man who knew the little moves of movies before there were, you know what I'm saying, talking, here, about here, here? He. Well. The man could punctuate with his eyes. I had not, as of yet, been introduced, yet, to the fine points of watching Kevin Spacey grow to 40 feet. And have eyes like pies were cloud cover, then it gets electric, little flickers. Then one of them tree flash neon day branches on the day sky, grey. Then dead, again, thick, and threatening. You want to date those skies. You want to make out with those eye skies. And you do not even bother with the wonder of why. Mr W? Similarly. He knew what moves the movies were going to make, even before movies. Before movies came, we always such a desire so. He made you feel you were the movie he wished he'd just seen to make him feel the way he felt looking at you with his eyes, just being in the room, in those offhand eyes. Like the desire for cine, before cine. Like the homeopathic healing of the medicine of cine we had long dreamed of, in. Offhand, and yet intense. Like a guy who pays you attention, and just breathes. Mr W, I hope you're out there this morning. We sure did. But the good times. So Mr W, this is going out to you. I been crawling up the street lately thinking of you, feeling myself in this heat like some kind of one hundred and seventy-six year old lizard keep you company, make Screamin' Jay look like voodoo took a long coffin antihistamine you been Barqing up the wrong root beer, dear, and so on, sitting here, let Mother Calamus attend you. Bertha Biotic. Biotic Bertha. Big Biotic Bertha of the Oitha and if were me and you knew you *were* me and I was you I could if I only would if *you* would – but would your I could be your one-syllable gecko, a geek on Ecology Street – Cala – Calamus Callipygous and her must-laden hair. Wake up Daddy Dust you've re arisen on Calamus Avenue. Dust my Calamus! Yeah, dust my little acorus and see how your broom might join in. The man was variegated! All stuff all mixed in and a songbird, songster stirred even those broomsticks to lean. Mary Mother Rogers and Out. Miss Storie.

Yes, I remember how Mr W back in the days of the Colonel – dear Colonel Colon (when he flirted with a Miss Tremont, he, for some reason called in their intimate moments, a Miss Fremont) – in those days there were so many coffee bars in the central business district and men all business in the city most commerce, mercy, Lord help me, have Mercy, get me some humidity, get me some of that it ain't the before I dry up and right desiccate to death, be some iguana's freeze-dried ride to space. Lord, get that humidity rising so that temp is falling, or we're going to be below the level of the sea, and there ain't going to be any sea at all out there, there, to see at all or what, what, tell me, and they did. Stood around and smoked cigars and everywhere they spoke in the papers of the rainy weather and Commerce and Coffee and the Blues on Love Street and how to find a cure for the rain and its resultant remitting feverish puddles. And I'm hoping for some fever rain myself.

Wake up those stumps.

Get out hobbling on those Civil War era rash underarm pit crutches or what. Get a rush on that lethargy, will you? Oh sleep.

Children, we're back here which you and me we've got a couple good ones today for you on Mother's Story Time. Oh Momma, you were never so good? – Right. La Mare. La Mamma's. Momma La's story time.

Welcome back to La Story Time. You like yesterday's? Me too. Now ... I'm not sure this is safe.... Now remember yesterday ... ____ & _____ were busy looking at that picture, remember....

S' just about that time all you bad boys and girls had your afternoon nap. Oh, don't tell me, I know what you're up to. Down, up to. Mother here's going to send you right to sleep with one of those bad – bad – slap your hand, girl – stories.

Hear that rain? Oh love that rain. Just pelting down. Just finished pelting down. Hand-crafted. I have always been fond of handmade artisanally elaborated rain. Now listen to mother. You just relax, now take your time. That's right. You don't worry about a thing. Mother's here. Mother Calamus is going to take care of everything here, with a little story time.

– Professor Regret
– Sweet Clementine Callipygous

– Rapture Alley, Rapture Annie
            Allie
            Aliea
            Alle
– Doctor Dusk
– Miss Slumograph
– Dog-Day Dug / Dog Day Doug
– Joe Plague / Plague Venus
spread that heat around baby –
– The Glamourama Hound
– Miss Fungus   Sweet Skin Callipygous
         Mould
– The Anchoritic Angel
with *The Anchoress*
Night Heart
This is NightHeart here whicha
Roo Too Loose / Miss Too Loose. Moss not loose enough.
Miss Loosey-Noosey I ever or is that for when it gets rain I hung
that time from the ceiling fan, trying to die, I ever tell you? I
was on HIGH 5, twirling. My knickers were in a knot, around
my neck, and twisted. I wished only for no regrets, but love.
   Just for you.
   From way back in the gone.
   The perps of these platters of the following vinyl crimes
stand accused of love.
   Miss Slumograph, Sweet Clementine Callipygous. The
Quim Kitty, Miss Kitty Quimola, Miss Kitty Quimville,
   Quimberg
   Kitty O'Quim
   Plague Karma
   Momma Plague
   Plague Momma
   – Miss Kitty O'Quim
   – Night Heart

– The Anchoress
– Miss Slumograph
– Sweet Clementine Callipygous
– Mother
– La The Professora / Miss Exito
                             Experience
professing
– The Blue Monk
– Miss Kitty Crepuscule
– La Glamourama
– La Professora
– Biotic Bertha
– Mary Rogers / Marie Roget
– Berenice
– Blue Berenice
– Mr W
– Mr W
– Eddie Lee
– Carrie Mocca
– Indigo Street
– Queen Calamus
Oh now here's some Sugar Boy Crawford on Chess 'No More
Heartaches' ......
   Mother Mercury.
   Miss Binge
   Sarah Tone / Cherie Tonin
   Sarah Tonin – Sarah Toenin
   Sarah Townin
   Oh a lot of fine sides today.
   For all we know, people, we are all God's side of fries, on
that.
   And we do not even know what side of heaven or what that
that is is at all if anything. Just going along, trying to shoot
straight. And we do not even know if what that that is we are

only a side of is anything. We can pray.

Out in the patio radio for the blinded me with its scent the jasmine beads all jazzing me.

And the kind of hanging old brown begging, oh, sense of the waters going to come, big, again some time. Mostly when cars are all rolled up right to the edge of the sunny beach. Enjoying some holiday long one. Some good one they are having. Blue skies and then the car's a boat, sometime. The roof is a ledge. The roof is where the garden deck chair is your boat shoes are boats the house hopes will float because it won't and the dog's off the chimney flying in a leap when it all is over, so unexpectedly. Such things.

Bird beak stars.

And the banana leaves asking for a little movement. None praying for calm.

And all elephant ears under the stairs.

Miss Nightshade
Miss Soul A Numb
Miss 4 O'Clock
Miss Weegee
The Philly Kitty   Broad Bertha
The Houndette.
Gothamology.
The Scoopette.
Scooperama
Mr W
Sarah Tone.

Jimmy Garcia! name of which the guy wasn't it, boxer who was killed and I remembering accurately in speaking of a Tyson 89 seconds, in 15, wasn't it or not 15 seconds, McNeely back you know my memory ain't what it used to be when I couldn't remember where I put it, but at least then I remembered I had a mind. Jimmy Garcia. You know that's who I think it was. Now, Señor Real. I did not ever hear goes to the fights. Maybe he does. He may go with his you know that, even after all these years, I do not even know would he have a even to say he'd wife I do not know. Saint Sweet was always interested in the public arena but now that I say it, I believe I did show Abraham some of my photographs of the boxers, I took, over time, in that great breath anticipation of movement so kin to the camera, why punches could be clicks. But Saint Sweet, above all, was a boxer, well a maven of the pugilistic science you might say, and his elevator kisses were so pugilistic.

Ere we're gone, baby. All gone. Miss Mould is back in your arms. Let's you and me make a piece accord. And we won't even tell the government. Let us lay down our little Adoration Station devotion-votes of evolutionary —— nada. Let us make little radio congress —— for the —— let us make of the night a congress. Let us make of the night a congress of love. Let us love the dark, in the night.

Now, Saint Sweet was a friend of mine. Saint Sweet was a friend of mine from up in New York City I met in an elevator once with Marvin Gaye in the room.

We cabbed up the side of the building.

The elevator had its taximeter on.

I saw him enter in from the distance from a large hotel lobby.

I liked how the man looked.

He gave me the erethric shakes.

I was working on mercury poisoning myself in various and sundry Sin Sunday positions doing a Mercury Sabbath on myself, when I saw the man from X a certain focal length made him so attractive to me, wanted to draw close. The room drew him near. The room took him along the lobby air to the elevator which I held open for him. Saint Sweet and I became ahems.

We said amens at the end of it, and it never ended, you see.

Child, you may have been there.

Elevator to life.

I had the mercury shakes, moment I see him.

I had the shakes of mad hatterdom, I see that guy's what? – brace, bracing, gate, along the, or dance, he was writing himself across the room with light. He was carrying that gold lobby like his life.

He was expresses himself with his exoskeletal movements as if he were a nervous migraine. His bones lit up like joints hopping with the happiness, Saint Sweet always seemed to have a coma on, but I called him Johnny. We were intimate before we met.

He had on medium-green pants. He had a lemon pale lemon green long-sleeved shirt. He had on brown boaters and no socks. It was winter. He looked like spring.

He came into the elevator and Marvin was on.

I was reminded that sexual healing was the homeopathic remedy for the lack of itself.

I was reminded that 'Sexual Healing' is the healing of the lack of the surfeit of the too much of the not enough blue sin of itself.

I was reminded that when the blues get in blue sin may be what cures it.

I was reminded of skirts. Of big bells to get up in and ding-a-ling-ling. Us? Saint Sweet and I? Don Johnny? And Marvin made a ménage à ascenseur.

And Marvin reminded me of my ecockology I knew once but forgot in some forfeiture come when your comeuppance seems to be more cum than thee.

I was so smug and Marvin desmugged me.

Much less a demi-God than a demi-urge of having a little Montecristo demitasse in lieu of to go to stay.

And Saint Sweet made three.

And the Montecristo demitasse made four, and the other one for he made five and we did jive with Marvin in our original Sexual Ecology. In our original brainless biotic beings.

Shucking off the antibiotic pride of maybe too lyrically poetic for our own good bad hearts and more into the swing. Back into the old original blue blues scholarship of Blauviolett letting our veins.

Some guys are a chord you spot from across the street. Seeming to hum the tune with their very aspect. Speculating it could be. Speculating it already is.

You have just stepped into the ongoing déjà vu of your being, seeing him, first time.

Saint Sweet stepped into the lift of my heart of the firsttime ascensor seeing him my heart had long scored itself with the tracks of him.

Don Johnny, Don Johnny, Johnny Sweet came in carrying for all the world his coma. The man sweat insulin.

I was working with the mercury, at the time, and I had that shyness commensurate with hatting and daguerreotyping.

I was fumed through with the very scent of the ascent of the sense of, Oh man.

I had a heart and it was outside my chest and it had an arrow in it and it was an organ.

I was a miracle of love.

I had left behind metaphor, image, symbols, simile.

I was love, I wore it outside, I wore a heart like a colostomy bag, I was alive.

I was living, yet, still, with my heart its real shape.

Do we need organs in it?

Or can they live without us?

Did my heart have a life of its own?

Did it live in an elevator with Marvin Gaye on, and the ecology golly gee in his zipped pants was panting to unzip quick-quick as we zipped up the hotel wall in gold. We were in a gold suitcase of love. We were in a bar at the top. We were inside a gold suitcase on a bar in a night. Of a bar at a night. In a bar, of a night. Of a night, at a bar, we were in a gold suitcase. And the gold suitcase opened. And we came out, small and music. Marvin was tucked inside little love pockets smaller. My hand felt a memory here. What was that tiny memory? Thinks: It was the curvy-curving up of the outer covering of the eggplant growing out. The: star – which was the old star flower husk. Is this a *family* resemblance – ? – And like falling notes scored on sheets of night music long drooped speakings came out things and spoke long skirts. And that little hanging tobacco thread off the side of the white skirt crinoline. Oh. And the crinoline skirt, back into the night was a faceless featureless little lizard lagarto lagartito sucking up to the stem and with little stub lizard arms prehensile and the long train skirt

Like a pointed shoe
in prayer
speaking out a long
punchinella trumpet
tongue with a morning
fly in one of the folds.
(one is
full)

Oh and there are about 50 trumpets beginning, and in all stages except full. Three days ago, baby, there were only pods hardly noticeable. Even though the tree is sickly looking. From bare buds to blooms in three days. Things move slowly but they grow fast.

You look at things a life and sketch them three seconds.

They say, How long did that take?

I say, It took a life, plus three seconds.

Night squiggle. Like a parrot green mouth open saying line-curve, line-L, line-curve-more-L-itself, L, line more nose on left and L like a shoe, at end, squiggle more square, definite curve and one more you-Miró-smile curve.

A plainer version.

Closed blurred out parrot-mouth. One swift line down, swift

line off that. Harder, faster. Line quick off that. Point up and line curve and line.

Parrot mouth open but closing, holding the trumpet bell skirt tighter, a line and sweet curve, off, line into it, line off of it, nice curve how it is, at bottom, loop, and around, line like facial expression line on a face, little one off like a dimple, line left like a mountain line, and curve-curve-curve-curve down like a mountain wall. V nib off parrot mouth.

In the smoky, a little *A Night in San Francisco* Van here now here, in the smoky, in the smoky morning, in the smoky morning, in the misty moonlight, in the misty moon, yeah hey all you nightbirds – all you night chirpers, welcome to we're back being – bathed in moonlight, baby – Dig that moon out there – in the meteor hours of meteor showers – You been rained on by this that meteorain yet, baby. Watch out for that meteor dust. Watch out carefully – for those angel souls. Yeah. St Jean used to write about all that – his angel souls and it sure enough it did – like a heart honking out its prayer, sure enough, in *On the Road,* 'And we saw New Orleans at night ahead of us with joy.' Man, don't you just know it. Don't you just love how preposi-tional our dear St Jean was. I tell you – The other day at dusk I got me into the Algiers ferry, for no reason 'cept to go across. And there was the river on the way to Algiers, there he was. There was St Jean's double. Maybe it was him. (Once in Philly City I saw Mr W board across to Camden.) There was St Jean's double I swear. But maybe I was thinking it was him. Maybe he came back. Maybe he he is with us yet. Maybe – maybe – oh baby, I can feel that morning raining down the golden after-noon all over the night – Betcha you can too. Yeah there he was – that fighter's nose – that been around the street, been around the ring couple-few times that Fero City alley sense of the pugilist not listing not even being standed-eight to the bar, or any place, just gorgeously combatant the way some guy's faces are *always* la lutta continua you know what I'm talking, so –

present. And at dusk for no reason. And at dusk the best reason is no reason 'cept crepuscule's falling, and that punched-in blue collar nose, and that pale manly male face and he'd had a close shave, and his hair was dark on his pale face and he had those child-gift manly eyes, babies – and face it, he's a hunk, boys, girls, he is. And there he was, with his leather jacket on in this heat, and looking out from the Algiers ferry just like he did in '5 . And it always being '55 and Mr W. And it always being '5_ and St Jean. I can hear them, now. I am inhaling their breath yet. And St Jean Louis there on the ferry with his heat leather jacket on there, there has that old French face there I know so well from those years in Montreal and those long summer days – yes, Ti-Jean, up in Tadoussac where once Basque whalers whaled over up those St Lawrence River long golden days, yes Jean-Louis, those golden late afternoons, oh yes St Jean, I knew your face, I saw that French-Canadian face, I saw you yester-day afternoon on the Algiers ferry when I was going across, I saw that beautiful pugilist nose. Hey baby, call me up – any-time. Anytime. Call me up. St Jean I want to hear your voice. Speak to me in English – your foreign language. Speak to me in your second language – your new language – the language of outside the house. (Speak to me of joy in your secret language you and your Momma used to speak in front of your wife.) Speak to me baby, in your second new tongue, speak to me St Jean, speak to me in these times. In these times of caution which truly does desire to be overcome by heart and in unbelief which can get awfully nasty but desires to believe in faith, St Jean honey talk to me in your second early tongue. Talk to me in your honey English darlin', your honey English of that strange delight. Talk to me in all your / Give me multiple prepositions, Jack baby, for I saw you up there on the deck beside me on an afternoon heat at – crossing over from the New Orleans side, tell me, baby, did you come back to visit yourself when you once stood looking over at another Miss and needed her so, tell me, baby, how long has it been?

And you who know early death so long in your life until you died all those years later hopped and shy, calling and wanting, the darling and the desirer, the wanton number of prepositions, the bagger of words in the strange second tongue, your heart was always in translation, baby, your heart was always the heart muse en français en anglais baby, my cabbage hipster my – put it this way, St Jean you kill me you do me good, Jean, —— tu me tues, —— tu me fais du bien, Jean you come back to me with your leather out-of-the-ring meditation on the ferry yesterday crossing over to see the President, yeah, to see the President's ghost, baby, did you come with me, did come with me son going to see the very President-to-be on Love Street. Did ya, didya, didya, didya, did you, did you, I think you did. Tell me St Jean it's been so long. It's been so long, honey, been so long. And Van Morrison put it something like this, In the golden afternoon, in the golden afternoon, in the golden afternoon, in the golden afternoon, and you St Jean, put it something like this too, '5 – in that letter to Neal Cassady, In the golden afternoon, oh yes – And you put it something like this, In the golden afternoon, oh yes you did, oh yes you did, In the golden afternoon you wrote, and you wrote, in the red afternoon, in Lowell and you had, and you had, and you have you have you have still all the best prepositions, all the best prepositions in the golden red blood utterances of your new fresh surprise second language which came to you when you first you came out off the old ancient sewing machine circle talk tongue and into the new school tongue of a new loverland you were born into strange and you were our living substitute for death. You were that blood replacement. St Jean good morning baby … … I'm breathing to find the sentence yesterday which excited me so in St Jean's letters but I popped a lens out of my glasses last night and I can't see but skewy. Is that dewy or savvy? Ken or icon? Cue or eau de valance or say what violence does it read ... ... morbid violence or ambivalence ... ... au eau or a venue ... ... grew ... gruel ... queue?....

St Jean my football-loving halfback, football playing quarterback looking adorer my jock jazzy Jean, Ti-Jean, thumbJack I saw your undershirt jacket and jeans on the Algiers ferry yesterday using your good old old football, just jazzing with that ball – Just holding your preposition there for me to see honey there is your mysterious word devotion returned to me – there in your adoration of the rhythm – there in your wide-eyed adoration of the rhythm, there holding that football like for all the world like an extra deciding will it go in or not to make the thing work. There sailing across Miss River holding on to that extra beat looking out for that sentence of the sky. Remember, baby, when you wrote 'I am, pops, that man'. And explained you stuck in, put in, that 'pops', so that that 'that man', wouldn't sound literarily 'that m-a-n-n' (so to say)-y. Listening to your always new to you second language like a throat visitor at the keys, baby, noting everything anything new like a young visitor from the ground. And you're right – You're right, right, right, right, right, right – baby. You are – I am the man, and I am, – , the man are 2 completely separate things – and the distance between these two material objects is one beat. You said forget the word skeptical and think – melancholy. You said forget _____ and think: _____ . You were present baby, you anticipated our skeptical – time. I am in that time, baby, I'm breathing it in my lungs. Oh but the low level ground ozone cruising Miss River with you and you took off that black leather jacket y football injuried back and you stood in your summer undershirt leaning over looking at the muddy river flow, and hey this one's going out to all those non-drivers like St Jean and me – and all the great non-drivers the world was just so busy rushing on by. Walking on those two pedal extremities walking down the street seeing things things – seeing doorways, seeing nightlights, seeing to look up that closed jalousie, baby, this is going out to all the windows on upper Ursulines, walking by those closed shutters, walking by those beautiful printed old rusty moulding peeling French dreams, walking by those coats of paint growing hair, growing shreds, walking by those beauties, just sitting waiting walking their coats of rust, just sitting there saying come back, come see me, come back, come see me, might still be here, might still be. Going out to that Chevy Impala 'saw parked looking so sweet in that full body rust coat sitting there on Dauphine, baby, sitting on Lord Dauphine looking like, hey baby, come back come back get me? Oh yeah, for all you out there dressed in that good nightcoat, dressed in that (rubber) metal gold glitter cool in the golden moonlight, in the afternoon of night, in the lower portion of the night, this is Mercy Baby coming out to you. This is for you St Jean back on Hildreth Street, Here's Van with 'Hyndford Street'. Yeah ... worshipping here at the altar of

words ... ...

(Mercy Nightshade.)

Worshipping here at the dark of words

For he who did worship at the

For he who dug the sacrament of the rhythm of how words are sounds. For he who did know exactly how many words of what beat to put together to make how many words exactly it took to make photography.

... Here, on Nightshade Street. Good evening, good night, good all night to you all joining us now – hope you got that night coat on. Poof! And what you say when that Miss Belladonna, Miss Beautiful Lady what was that – poof! What was that sound effect there you're playing around with.

Why boys and girls, babies and nabies, boobs and bobaloos, scoots and scoobie doobie doobies that was night, the very first photographist – telling – yew! Being naughty – Oh night's seen it all, night. And those things they call stars? Hey that's the aftermatter of your eyes. That's the sun glow, the post-flash, the eye strain-bop of that left hook floored you. That's night poof powder, that's night's flash pan, oh baby you caught now. You on that plate you are – history. You'll be some fine find some yard sale garage junk junkyard backyard afternoon day, times to come. Okay let's do it – Three in a row.

'Carrying a Torch' Van again. Let's do King Bee 'Sly Hypo' and how's about we throw in for good measure '200 Lbs. of Joy' with Mr Willie Dixon ... ...

Okay that was joy on the Mason and Willie Dixon line with a caller from says that should be 2 point 2 into 200 equals what was that again darling, kilos, I suggest a nice Datura Asthma Lights might calm those death threats down, which further to it, caller says if Mercy here do not stop talking about how we are bound to that green mouldy veil, caller's, 'I'll kick up my little muffet tuffet carry-on's got a bomb I intend to leave on the radio station step, we are very important people, do not call us mould, I am changing the world today,' caller says, 'So just stop saying I am a moth-eaten veil, or I'll blow you up.'

And I said, 'Darling, do me that big personal favour of go jump in some chocolate pain soup.' I said, 'Maybe, darling if you apply to the government, you might get a grant to bomb. But don't forget that ticking clock, darling,' I said. I said, 'Darling, I have heard the likes of you leaving suitcases radio stations, and shuls, north and south.'

And just for good luck, I rubbed me my mouldy grub shroud all over the phone. Just to get a little ——— : LOVE, down the line.

I said, 'Darling, you don't behave, I'm going to lock you up in my vinyl morgue gown.'

So in mind of that in mind of maybe later we'll put on a little bit of 440 Kilograms of Joy – oops! Honey you just doubled your syllable weight, you ballooned up from a slim 200 pounds to a real grossero 440 kilograms, let's take us here a few little clouds of ounce joy with that was the Mighty Torch Carriers with 'Van Again', King Buzzard and the Harpos with 'Don't Buzz Your Quaker Bonnet (or Leave My Bee Bonnet Be)', so honey this is going out to all you centimetre sniffers, some Miles, with *Bitches Brew* peeping and no purpose in the pink I'm just itching to get some of that ever see over at that K & G boil balm looks like castor wax on wheels, yeah like a roll-on record player wheel-on expandable case of ——— : Love, but man way it smells makes how to looks look like it was Miss Boil Balm of the back seat velour snatch you still dreaming on, these years later, back of that old or was it a Mark V or an old Olds '88 you moulded your old oldie right into that sugar plate, or it might have been something, or some other or-else beating down on you, anonymously. That caller's nose was so out of joint sounded like there was a major break at Angola and the noses ran. Like those smells crawled in to such a small drawer made Sing Sing look like, Oh my, up there up past the many high floors of Charlie Parker, to the rooftop parking garage, to jump. Make Alcatraz look Jazz Island on the rocks in the misty dreams of them Jimmy Stewart eyes on the sidewalk hanging wearing 2 foot casts. Oh don't you love to make pretty things even prettier. Not too pretty mind. Just put in at the station with your red dress on a ticket long as you are tall. Okay, for all those babies thought better of the thing and just relaxed, laid back, did a little can-can at Club Can Coma and wandered back into that old Bar El Ax, bringing you a now just lay back inside that banana leaf, and let God smoke you … … ….

I do not know much, been so busy staying home, tatting my noose.

I swear to God, you're going to miss me baby. Maybe even just one sound.

And hey Jean-Louis you want to honk me in honk blue joual hey my little thumb / well you go on right ahead, you want to kill me with a little Canada honk honk me honey honk me and bonk me and boink me and oink me and oil me down. Kill me with a Québecois, do me good any good godly bodly bodily body-part god! Lord! Lord! Lord! Lord! Lordy.

Lordy Lordy Lordy Lordy Lordy, man, baby, boy do me with your undershirt's your bod, your bodly bid, your biddy, do it, man, oil me and spoil me and honk me and bonk me borksville baby, do me good any way you so desire, Here's some Bobby Blue Bland with 'I'll Take Care of You.' And hey since we're talking to that star cutting contest up there the sky after Bobby Bland let's do Van ...... Junior Wells. First time I heard Bobby Bland do this it's those just you never mind what I was doing there old late nights – remember babies sin in old Gottingen Street those old port nights when it got all up in the inner harbour all orange with rain like Marlon Brando was made particulate matter and liquefied. And came, across the water, like he and his rental decor just poured, before he sat with his wife, and he said, Why did you kill yourself, baby, what could have driven you to take yourself away from me, and never tell me.

I have wondered, in the desert hours, about those yellows of the *Lasts*. Have you ever noticed, baby how *The Last Temptation of Christ*'s gold and *Last Tango in Paris*'s gold blend. You could have Willem damn Dafoe climb down off that cross in that last 20 minutes before the last and go to Paris from Morocco and need an apartment to stay in outside the central core and be in that winter gold, cold, so strange and dry as night comes, like the desert. In the low humidity of nights when the humidity is low, do you ever notice the sky, regardless, remind you of some long ago lost blue cold desert night. And that gold dying feeling. He said I don't know why you did it. And we don't. We can never know. To know why one dear to you died by their own hand is as little available, to us, as to know a time past, by looking up the customs.

I have often thought, from time to time, what if the assholes we read in the paper, today, had asshole ancestors of yore.

What if oldy-timey tiny minds got in the paper to blow farts, as they do today, baby, in this our nonce time?

And if our la-di-da noncey turns yap on, why in yoresville ain't they?

How is it we take the past to have a venerability our vulnerability, of now, dispermits us and just like, I'm, 'Oh yeah right, says who, "Blowhole"?!'

What if who is listed as research found for the Then, stood apart from the Love Street, of then, as the writer using them, does now?

It has, of course, been many years already, more than a decade, since first I saw in the papers of record, 'Now that typewriters are extinct,' and I sat down at my trusty companion Mr Smith-Corona (as Miss Underwood looked jealously on) and (the Misses Underwood, in truth; such things do go on) and promptly write a letter to the editor, on that. I ran out of typing paper that very day. And at my local stationer's they were sad to inform me that once again, someone had got the last of the typing paper, which was always gone.

As the years went by, I noticed, 'Now that Extreme-Love typewriters are extinct,' and 'Now that nobody uses an Urlines love pencil, any more,' and in my venom I broke more than one 2B or 3B scrawling and scratching all over the newsprint messages with my long black lead.

This led me to surmise, perhaps in the 100 years and 200, when we are seen as both fools and sages, we might be seen as sages where it said, 'Now that Saint Love typewriters are extinct,' and 'Now that nobody uses a Slumograph pencil anymore,' and fools where we said that all those members of the Compositae family such as echinacea weakened you, as did the ginseng. It is not unknown that in the journalistic trade, practitioners of said trade are known to live and work a lifetime without ever seeing the outside. Some, released early, are bewildered and become suitably wild, as befits freedom, to discover a strange and marvellous creature called Saturday night.

I have always liked the handmade. I like the old-fashioned things. They are always modern. Technology will come, technology will sleep, but there will always be hanging.

I hung, not long ago. And some damn listener arrives at the studio, to help me. God help the leisure class. To sui onto your host, as you would sui unto thyself only thy Thee just cuts, jumps suiship, last latebreaking nooses which holds and *you* off, and your sui helper talks about it. Suicide is like sex. Some do. Some watch. Some do. Some help. Hopped off her opium bed, knocked me up here in my slave quarter redo, tries to talk me off.

It's my red wagon of dying, this yob off they hear me hanging myself on the air wants to help me. I'm, like, 'Let me hang in peace.'

She and or he's like, 'Let me talk you down.'

I'm, like, 'Talk yourself down because baby way I see it, There's you, me.

'There's you, me.

'There's you, my red wagon, me, you trying to get in my red wagon okay it's a wheelbarrow.

'There's me, you, my red wheelbarrow, William Carlos Williams, depends on, makes you do the math.'

I believe helping the lonely to die is today's what the genteel do, to have an educational experience.

To help We the Lonely assimilate to heaven.

Peace was the love we ignored. Once, we danced with peace late at night and whispered love talk.

Once we did not care what piece of peace we put back in the back seat of that Cadillac car, peace just so's baby we could get down and lick you, love you, ask you why you died, what could we, what did we do wrong?

We used to glam in houndy to the smoke partitions made even the smallest place seem much larger, as any of the better garden landscapers will advise you, and smoke was our trellising, then, about 2-3-5-6 feet in created that little framing to look through all blue and kind of mysterious as to what lay beyond could wait we kind of hung on to in that peripheral sweat.

In the dark like cabs all hung.

In pressed right up close to some sweetie pie hand right there and bobby blues coming out of where blues comes out of some hour past any hour and you're just so grateful to dance oh baby when we were only 24 hours a day and there was all the time in the world – and I'm still bearing in on Bobby Blue Bland today all these decades later as you will too when the end of the world does not come and we walk through scorch prayers hoping for those bespoke fallen puddles. Okay.

Once, in my dreams, I blew the silver harp peace was. I was the reed for peace. I was the reed's sweet agency. I ministered to the keys of peace we knew the black night was falling. I ministered to the holes of peace in the many keys of darkness. Daddy Dark, you called me. I was once a thrall of peace.

And then I took peace for granted oh baby.

And we did and oh I did I took peace for granted I did not even go out at night stalking around, peeping, get a good look in on peace's sex hots. I forgot how hot peace was, when relaxed like Adolph reinvented sexophones, each night. Yeah, I said to peace, yeah.

The sound of peace is not diplomacy.

Peace is not kept by diplomats.

Peace is kept by passion.

The sound of peace is not consensus.

The sound of peace is that momentary breath pause you keep going back to rub just that spot where Coleman Hawkins is blowing 'Blues for Yolanda' and just in that momentary instant where Ben Webster comes in to blow his entrance no peace more seductive has ever been blown.

Peace is not everyone agreeing.

Peace is love.

Which excludes so much.

Here's Bobby Blue Bland with 'I'll Take Care of You'.

Yeah 'I'll Take Care of You.' Anytime Junior anytime Bobby baby Van anytime. Okay. Now out of that pods' mouth, out of that nightshade pod, out of that puffing up pods like the cousin hey eh of a green bean and those scallopy familiar family leaf I would now lief get down on my knees to peace, and beg. Yeah, cousin to green bean those human green pods with their night tubes, with those appearing green lemon skirts hey eh oh baby boy of that nice eh lemon pale green, don't you ever wonder how those puff green pods of that do not misstate me just date me Datura Tree come out with all their night white night skirts yeah and a couple days later that pod baby and that night skin full over white green white lemon green nightskirts. Baby am I the skirt for you? Baby am I the morning poison skirt for you? (Oh: 'It's a Man's World', then we heard 'For Men Only', 'Advice (For Men Only)', two of my alltime favourites. How can the trumpets of white nightshade Datura dates dates of being dated by Miss Belladonna sweet Lady Night come on, so slowly, and so fast they are gone. One day, not there, next day, gone. One day not met, yet, nor even on that street alone has been sighted, then a couple three days later after the fullness fades, they go. It is these brief things which return we remember. One On Street, one corner of ON and IS, baby, I have, on occasion, found myself wandering along ART ST. in a heart trance, until I was found in the 1000 block of ST. ART just riverside of ST. S IN. I love them cave days. Three days, then days, it is over. We are one scratch from the outset. I'll use a stub and a paper bag. Let me make you a nice nigh nightshoe of paper you can use. I have been palped by love, in my dreams.

Hey, this is Miss Nighshade speaking to you. You going to keep me some company here while I spin you a few little trumpets and just went out and picked uh-huh right off of my back

night here little little little little little little little night Nightshade tree.

Miss Soul a Numb Miss Soul Numb –

Miss Eggplant, Potato, ... (Photo?). . . .

(One of them when are we I ask you you're right a caller
wants to know when we going to do a whole Doc Pomus hour
answer is it's about time . . . or . . .)

. . . Three in the morning. . . .

The Golden Eternity.

And if you're looking for poetry babies, if you're looking for
a poet honey pet who's got some nice throat honey pots you
might bring your just you never mind on and up and into a cut
try Van the Man talking poetry. I am hoping that, in time, he
will be nominated from the Country of Love to be who had
touched us, in verse. He has never held us distant.

Baby I am thinking of you, now, before your sweet premature
grey hair was blown up in that misplanted mine, and we used to
sit up on St Charles Avenue in that sweet old big old Columns
Room Number 16 bathtub. Mr Jefferson you recall yourself of
late now to me of late I find myself thinking. I remember our
ménage in the bathtub. Our ménage du bidet. You, me, your
cock and okay, Mr Webster. You, me. Me, you – Mr Jefferson, Jeff
Junior, and Mr Webster in the *Soulville* days when he came without Hawkins. I remember when we sat inside. In the hot blue
days, the dark is so fine for contemplation. In the dark we
poured out from the vat-sized bottle the suicide-strength 'Lord's
Blood' shingle-soothing sauce. You were fine, baby. You were
fine. In the soft green long lost gone green willow hangs of spring
catkins on you, in those ponds, in those ponds. In the triangular
mud love, out there. In the long river land of skies the mountain
country clouds so big can come to resemble. Homeless in the
poverty of my heart, I have loved you.

We made whoopee and whoopee loved it.

Baby 'The Touch of Your Lips'.

It was spring and everything was new and about to be over. We rode pink rivers down the tracks. The mist was hot flood air coming. It was the grey hot spring presage of hurricane time. The clouds were close as covers. They were tall.

The clouds always were as close as brick buildings. They were the sky architecture of God.

The city was low and cottages. The sky was the higher fold.

I sat with you here on Love Street and I packed you in my suitcase.

The thing which was you was the pocket watch with you on the other side of the clock.

The thing which was you was the picture I shot of you, after you died.

Saint Sweet in the elevator reminded me of you. He laid me down when the doors closed in the elevator. Nothing would heal us sexually but 'Sexual Healing'. Nothing will cure the blues but the blues one more time.

These are the palmy days.

We are in heaven, right now.

You were an illuminated dayenu, in the bed.

It sufficed there, with you, in every moment.

My diaphragm seemed alive. I had a different breathing. Love made me breathe, awhile. Ane hwile.

The cicadas drove the streetcars up and down St Charles.

The cicadas moonlighted by being big spies in at the windows of hotel rooms, trying to peep in those close shutters not knowing day or night but for the sound of them big as the streetcars they drove.

We came north to New Orleans, from the southern wars.

I have a vet heart.

I have it still.

People, I am with you veterans. I am one of you. I am one of you. I too have seen war. I too have returned in great bewilderment at to what is this world we live in, and do I even any more, or did I, even, in first place ever, speak the same language, as they who take peace so for granted. They do not any more, any more, want to go meet peace illicitly to dance close and reacquaint that preciousness of how it feels to sweat close and be thankful. Give thanks to God for being blessed and able to dance at all. This thing dark is so unnameable. The days were thunder and felt like clubs.

Loving you, baby, was like loving war, in peace.

Howling zygotes but happy not too tearful just weepy, sick inside but not saying much as war teaches you it is much more in the faces. Is along the lines of how words are so insufficient.

It is those confident who think, if you work at it, humans can communicate, who make you want to die. I have desired this. And even quietly when I loved you. And I loved you baby. I did not know how big a room could be, or how the small space of it could take every square inch and make it a collection of moments. We breathed time. If I thought we could communicate by words, I would have hung myself, long ago.

I fear there may be a plague of optimists, out there.

And Saint Sweet, Saint Sweet was no optimist, baby. Though he did remind me of you. He was a true blue, tried and true pessimist, and so sensual, and sexy. Optimism kind of, you know takes the K-Y out of the situation.

And I've been longing for a while to have that loving, again, a war vet seems to have at his disposal so often it seems strange. It much resembles hypoglycaemia, to me.

Yeah. In just that way of air of knowing. Just to have a war vet say, Yeah, like a human hypoglycaemia attack, coming. That urgent rush, that sugarlessness of insulin shock in the body cells you feel, that sweat, that coma coming. That sense of death, at every moment, which makes a human sexy.

I have met men who have gone to war, and lived from it, and they exude this sexiness of they have not left yet at all, yet, yet they have come home, already, and died. They are packing for that long gone voyage, on which the plane will crash. And it is sexy.

I have met men who much resembled, just in their going about their ordinary everyday affairs, that they were perpetually on that last day before leaving, doing that smooth going out, doing stuff, being that stranger walking down the street, giving off that sweet: I am the unlikelihood of me.

Let me be solvent unto heaven. Oh Lord.

Lord, the state.

The state paid handsomely those who, on the state's behalf, advised the way was to go out, be out, take advantage of all the opportunities, and celebrate that we no longer had to stay home, alone, and work in the moss closet, or the desert gold.

And after a while, you noticed, this was true.

We did not have to stay home alone behind the rainy window, or the Tstorm building up or the cumulus all accumulated up eating their way through sky.

There were many opportunities and a multitude of options of the ways in which each of us could follow the role models who had chosen now that it was open to us the many more ways then available, to us, previously, not to be Miss Dickinson.

Rather than the more limited selection of previous times, we had a broader base of technological methods not to be great.

Where so much depends on a teleological totally illogical often unsupportedly meteorological astronomical lunatic feeling, one moon.

Baby. Our hearts are mouldy veils. We have been shaped out of brick shadows.

We are meant to stay small, and be worldly as small moss bits of aerial views. To forget the going and moulder.

Our hearts are so secret. Who knows these things we wish to know? Who even knows where are the doors to them? I was always just looking for that little blue love sanctuary with you. Baby I did not desire much.

And when I came to the art made of ground bones of meat made liquid on rags in order to be sheet music for breathing the air of musical tones up into the eyes, hearing with your irises, and I said, 'You know you know what this seems flat to me,' I was told, 'It is not flat, they give away a lot of money to the needy.'

And when I said, 'I thought that was called being a menschlich human being. I thought that was being a human being,' I received no answer. And when I said, 'I thought that was, you live, that was the law,' I received no answer. When I said, 'I thought you did that as a matter of course, and then you began,' I received no answer.

And when I said, 'This seems all mind, and so little heart I see in this here book on the page,' I received no answer. I received the answer, 'It is not flat as a pancake, they give away a lot of money to the poor.'

And when I said, 'I thought that was what we were born to do, regardless,' I received no answer. And when I said, 'Why would they go into a job which requires a keen sense of music, of dance, of movement, and there seems to me, here, on the page, none of it,' they said to me, friends said, in response, 'They give a lot of money away anonymously nobody knows about.'

And when I said, 'I thought that was the way.'

And I say this to you friends, today.

People,

But baby I would trade all your gelt for one true word.

But baby I would trade all your empathy for one true song.

For one heart which down baby down bends down on bended knee in adoration of one extra beat.

Which is down on its knee in alley adoration for the misused beat.

Who knows that Jean-Louis meant oh I am so tired, lately, baby of this life, so beaten down by it, in original rust.

Oh honey I was looking to who handcuffed themselves and ball and chained their ankles and strapped themselves in to that sentence. Listen to your mother here. Here's the bit. Wake up! Git down, doggy. It's pit bull to lower terrier by tonight. It's looking a little shepherd blowing in from the east. We might see some bird-dogs by breakfast. But basically we're looking at we're going to be seeing keep that muzzle on by midday that heat's going eat off your face.

Look, you want to plead down in your sentence, you do it.

Maybe you want.

Maybe you want that sentence shorter by yay much but maybe you want it longer by yonly yay-ay it's, somehow, to say the way it only occurs to me, now, I remember, and recall how was it the morning before yesterday you know did you ever have the feeling you wanted to ask did you ever wake up in the morning, knowing what you knew in your sleep, walking inside words, which was, what you knew in your sleep came to you when you awoke and lay in the dark with your eyes closed, that the shape of ache is note, which somehow leads me to say stay out of my graveyard wax I'll let you suck my big marlin monrowy white cloud tower Miss Heap skirt if only you would let me be your frail to you, and scat Roman Vishniac testosterone blowups, so resemblings of the stars, in the blue night and in the night the night, no is not, the night in the night is no, the night is no fugitive, and the night is no fugitive, and the night is no fugitive, the night does not go, the night never goes, the night does not run away, the night is mordant, and inordinately in the ordinary weirdness of light when it is that indigo blue, the most material power of the hour of blue does unrest you like a magenta mogul in a cyan green vice-verse and more sighing than soughing oh how sweet it is in indigo dreaming for the night is our mordancy, the night eats us and oh yes it is, and the night eats away, the night stays, the night stays, the night stays, and the night's own stays say, The night is no fugitive and the night is indigo, and indigo, baby, is its own intention and it does not escape, night is indigo, plain and, lonely, it seeps, it soaks, it is us, life, for it, it soaks it seeps to soaks us in, it seeps it soaks, it soaks it speaks spokes right into us night little twitches of how fine it all could be, in starlight, oh light: night is indigo in our cellular composure and old night all night composes our molecules and makes it so pretty it all seems all right even you just go ahead and have that cry, baby, for we have been there, before, even if not so, to say it, yes and yes, it and yes oh it and yes it is, not so sour but pretty as pretty eyes night makes at the sky to take it and make it pretty forever, a picture, sweet as Teddy Wilson, sweet as Teddy Wilson making stars at the keys on the indigo, intended, as I will, sky, be your intended, one day and let me tell you this, people, people, children, friends I want to tell you this, walk with me a while, I hope you do not mind, excuse me, friend, pardon me? if I walk with you a while, friend, and I hope you do not mind, as we walk if I tell you: I walked out into the desert, I was prebetrothed to sky, I was already married and for night composes us and I knew that, but friends, I did not know, until I had seen it, and I saw it may I say, that night, that: night is the indigo composition of our cells, baby, night, like indigo, does not go, always stays and yes it does, it does, it always stays and always been the way, always will be, always will be that way, nothing changes, there is no progress, oh but my the sky does ring changes like little delicatenesses so fine and little Teddy Wilsons make all kind of prisoners of love, up there, on the sky, feeling, see? feeling that, you see, you thought it would do shorter, but now you're in it, you want it longer, that sentence or the sense it, how it seems much longer too and how when it gets started it is one of those affairs which just does not know how to put a fool end to itself it is just such a little fool for love of the continuous, baby, you might want a longer sentence and you might want a sentence with just that extra little thrill and yes, just that little extra thrill, yeah, so you waste a line, waltz along, be a fatologist, you want something, something, yes, yeah and yes it is and it's true more than you'll ever know, and you'll never know, only your heart knows, and it's not telling just yet, there is no telling where your heart goes, but baby pay close attention to your sentence, it's your sentence you got to bargain with, listen to your mother here, listen to mother, talk to your sentence, don't be a stranger, if you are a stranger to your sentence, your sentence will know, and it will be over between the two of you, gone cold, when you come home at night from all kind carousing, talking about how you love it, sad not to be loving it, but being as you are doing the more important, apparently to you (to you and your sentence), talking about it you could have been spending that time talking to it, it will go cold on you, it will stop breathing, but listen to mother, talk to your sentence, see if she barks back, and what about the great power of blue, and what, what tell me, tell me what what what what what, and what about the healing power of the blues baby, in lost los blues, in less les blues, in dire die blues, yes what about the healing power of *love* I mean does the sentence sing or and yes does the sentence sing or what, or what baby, does it swing it's okay baby you just have yourself that cry that things are, that things are, that things are, that words are, when words are they are things, leave off that literal baby, leave the literal way way way way way way out on that littoral baby and that thing that, that that-things-are, if you love thing, love thing, if you love things, love things, love baby, strut out into the incarnational vision, Big Baby step out into — things! so you strut out into the incarnation vision, step out into the power of the material world, this thing which is, this world this wonder into this indigo night we go and dig it, git-go, going into its intention I was a bigamist to mortals, after I went out into the desert and found I had been married to sky before I was born, and my wedding was the first time I saw it, I was the bride of sky, step out into the mist, I was sky's lover, step into that misty wet material incarnate world, step up on those clouds' steps, I was the sky's little lover, I was the sky's bride, I was the bride of sky, first time I saw the sky in the desert, I came out into the Stations of Humidity, and I was dry, I married sky, once, I had so many second and third fourth, I even married Number Five, and none of them knew when I looked in their eyes, I was always looking over their shoulders into my eyes into the night of indigo, for indigo is the power of intention, indigo is the power of the material power of the material world, us, there is an indigo which went and thralled us, there is that indigo to which we are born, thrall, step out into the midnight, step out into the jasmine, step out into the whiteness, step out into the stars, steps out into the little bird beak starlight vines crawling all over the atmosphere so thick like sounding from the sea the foghorn, step out into that white blinding scent, step out into the night and the sea up there, step out into the midnight, time of day the human species is scared both of the river and the lake might B and E your heart honey, I know, it's so lonely, in there step out into the heartbreak and the heart loss, baby, I am with you, I married sky one day, and then I came out into the darkness, and in the desert the sun rose like it was a sunset and I saw all the sky lit up like mountains was Mark Rothkos, and Lord, *I knew* I was alive, I was the — intention itself, I was indigo's — intention, indigo went and gave birth to me while I was asleep and dry, I was indigo's baby, I wanted so to be indigo's baby, and be cradled by indigos, be sounds' baby, at night, step up on that cloud cover baby like the clouds was the stones down to the bottom of the sea all rocks, step out into the indigo night, baby, with me, step out into that glitter rain raining down right now inside of you, step out into all things things strewn step out into one lonely silhouetted bench in three lines drawn at sunset at Zabriskie Point I have often seen, in my dreams again, when first I was born in the salt and it was all one rock high grey wall and one small on the high rock grey wall toothpick bench and that toothpick bench was a universe of love, past Zabriskie into Zounds Point, it was us, in a matchbox, I was moss once, I was the aerial view at my own feet down below my toes, I was that moss nub I walked down to the bottom of the ocean and sat on that one bench, and I said, I do believe a matchbox would hold my clothes, I do believe I tore my heart out for a miracle of love and I put it in a matchbox which I found in Miami at a Camel stop which had all of Miami in the matchbox and inside that little matchbox Miami was the Harlem Square Club 19 and 63 and inside that small Harlem Square Club of Miami in 19 and 63 was Sam Cooke and Sam Cooke sang, 'Standing here wondering, would a matchbox hold my clothes,' and baby, the going is easy, the going is right, it is right because it is easy and it is easy when you forget that is going at all to even be right, baby I walked down the stone steps and everything was beautiful, and Roland Kirk had three clouds in his mouth and he was amped (and Jackie Wilson sang), and he was hurt, (and Jackie Wilson sang and Jackie Wilson was shot) (or was that a heart attack) and I had been in a lifelong ball and chain sentence, to the sky and the sky put on its red dress and came down to the station, and I said to myself, Baby strut (And Jackie Wilson sang 'FOR YOUR LOVE') out in those crepe myrtle laden banquettes, step out through the purpling hibiscus strewn in amber beer-bottle glass, step out (and into: JACKIE WILSON sang: *'For Your Love'*) (and out into where:) Jackie Wilson sang 'For Your Love,' down into the canyons where highup mountain views down are the view into time, and up high in the desert we are looking at space but most important to our heart, we are looking down at the shadows of time where concrete things are time, in mind, down into the long shadow valleys, where 'FOR YOUR LOVE' is *'For Your Love'* is 'For Your Love' is for your love I am hoping, sometime, into the purple and red neon shortlings on that sidewalk in the roomy city, step into the secret grotto of lung snug asthma pie, wide out into the muddy Miss Water all naked with no clothes on baby and lay back in the golden afternoon on your favourite little latte coffee, go jive with your corner barista, go swim in out never that hung in loose cypress pine, in the brick folding, in the muddy lounging, in the peel preparation, in the wet old eyes, in the green rust hair, in the old ways, in the new ways, searching for the new, searching for the new, searching for the new, searching for the yeah new, the yeah new yeah the new yeah the look for the new, the able-bodied look the noble look the crippled looking, the looking, the looking, the looking, the seeing, the seeing, the seeing, the scene, the old scene, the new scene, any scene, any scene, any scene, any scene baby, any scene, just, yeah, search for that – sentence, for that one right word, for that one true syllable, in that true heart percussive percussion tells you that one true beat, in that one line sentence, in that one rhythm, yeah, I mean baby just that mumble and make it blue, just a that mumble make it blue in hoodoo voodoo any you do please, keep your eye on the sentence, speak to the sentence, someday baby, someday baby, someday baby that sentence speak to ——— you.

Baby.

I will be dead, before this is ended.

I will hang myself in your sight.

I will hang myself, in your hearing.

I will pledge my love to the word.

I will be faithful to music.

I, long before I was born, and found I was already married to the sky, I opened my eyes, I found I had been married, before that, to the music. I found that Mr Sky was in truth and I myself did not even know it, until, just, I swear, just this one moment, I just find out, and truth is you and me find at the same time, I found out Mr Sky is Husband Number Two and Mr Music, I find out I had been married before I was married before I was born, it seems even I myself did not know I lie now you know what you got to redo the math on those previous hitches. Husband Number Two he was Husband Number 4 and Husband Number 3 did not know what husband and did not, 'I don't care what Husband' – number 'Number 2 says you I say you sound like Blobby Boo Band' is now Husband No. 5 and Husband No. 4 and Husband Number Never-Mind is Husband two more.

Some days you wake up and you and you had 2 more husbands than ever even ever *you* dreamed of. Some guy's calling in from the left luggage depot, 'We got a make on the, you come down and gander this cock chart see which one matches up with the penis of your dead husband,' and you're ID'ing a guy you had an apparently with. Back in them incrediblies when the time of 'Hey looks familiar was he the guy I went to some delicious delirium with once way back in or is that that other not so bad to tell you the truth, or the yeah going by, handsome stranger looking in that shoe window to see me and my reflection shooting him gandering me in the name of those pretty leather loafers. Much like soft slipper gloves.'

I love this so much beautifu.

But I am going to kill myself.

I am making you that promise.

I am giving you my word.

I will hang myself by the ceiling fan.

Alone.

By myself.

I will murder me.

Premeditated self-homicide. I like the word meditate. I like to meditate. I like to meditate on killing. I like to meditate, in advance, about murdering. I like to think deeply, in a religious desert, about killing. How killing is two, and kill one. How Sin is one, too. I believe you should meditate every day. I believe daily meditation is good for you. I believe meditation is a good thing. Meditate on killing yourself. Yeah, I like to practise meditation. To premeditate murder.

Yeah.

I will murder me.

I will kill me.

Suicide.

Three syllables, no help.

2

.. .. Baby, I've been trying to draw you the shape of my love for so long now. I've been making of the night sheet music on which to draw those Datura skirts, and make you you know the music?

There has been something about just that little part where it lifts. Like an entrance, you know into a club, in that first note there's a sense.

Some nights, that ———

——— all streets are 'Perdido'. In great anticipation of when's Ben walking in and you want to be so close with him, you call him.

'Why, my lands, Mr Webster,' ——— That bass just kills you, in the wait. Then Ben's in like the open hand of the open door of the big fat sack you carried, baby, up that mountain. Just before you.

Go, and, 'I think I'll hang myself, "Hang on, don't," comes in the call of one more advising ghoul helper,' yourself, everything's funny.

And let me tell you this.

Baby, do not ever.

Get the mandarin mainstream mixed up.

With chance. Do not go mixing.

Up that art politician.

With the underground. Don't let them fool you. Your heart knows best.

Yes. Heart rest.

Hey you. Heart knows that a thing a year a week an hour in advance of the extreme foreground is not the underground of love you have long looked for. In the night you have been in the desert. You have longed, baby, to be a portrait of that love. You have longed to be made a portrait of your loneliness, so they could tell. Let me be that limnist for you. Let me limn you with my love. This is Soulville coming atcha. I plead guilty to loving Ben Webster. That man is a hot tub to write a bath about. Could I tell you about that skirt I desired to draw for you.

It's that little nicotine thread at the lift, of it, I so desire to draw you. (To tell you a thing which if words could say it, — *oh* —) –, and all we had *if* to do was find the time to write it, the world would be an allée of big old shade trees with a hundred humans hanging from it, all writers. It is this music. I'm creeped out by books which say they're about evil, and do not even — scare you. —————— the Devil loves the ironic. ———— No three-headed one-eye each reed sax, He. The devil-ironic never touches the heart, and that is why the Devil loves it. Oh the belated beloved things we so wish now to love, close up and gone. .. .. blue. Like ——— yeveryday mordant indigo my habitual. Sky was my habit. The light coming down on darkening has so much made me want to draw. Uh-huh. Oh yeah.

a little light tower, blue.

The light close when the clouds are the mountains seas dream of. Baby, get under that cloud cover, and sweet problem-solve sweetmeats with me.

Heaven's light church out there happening, wake up tow-heads and tugs. Lug your guts up to that porcelain cloud nearby.

Wash them grubby paws there on old Sin Street. I mean. It's

all means. Let me be your little problem-solver, for love, you have been mine, for me. Who has not been a fool for love? Who has not gone to a work of art, with such hope, and felt betrayed I'm talking to all of us, baby. You are mine. Speaking like the.

Time is love, and 6 seconds is plenty.

But like they want to *tell* you about time, as a, never mind. But not make time with you, in love-making. There's always time for rain.

Freshen up that white space. You ever notice the air in some books is the words are there, but the white space is lacking the music. I was always looking for them kerteszische raindrops. I liked to check in on the Czech of it, and just trance how letters were like photos when you did not know the language, and the air came through. (Sometimes it has seemed.) Honey, I am breathing fat clouds out at you. I am breathing the many towers. I have breathed the skin of the rain.

This is Mercy, in the Darkness. Let me intimate with you. Let me be Those Big Cine Lips. Let me talk you like that big terra cotta red mouth. Yes. Let me be your rouge pulp. Yes. Yeah – yes. Let me be your red gloss rain. Let me red rot, in your ear, so sweet, you want it, lasting. Let me be rouge rot, baby. Let me the red rot rain. Let me the red rot network. I am, baby. I am. I am for you, baby. Baby, for you I am that. Rosa roja. Not too luxe, but just lujo enough. I luxuriate for you. Let me be every xxx of love you once dreamed of is now that sidewalk graffito tells your story, when it says to you in that asphalt I NEVER TOLD YOU I HAD A CRUSH ON YOU OR ANYTHING. Let me be that crush, who never told you. But yet you so suspected. Let me be your rainy stretch skin, black vinyl highway, long black vinyl record-length coats, slick rainedon grooves up and down my body, stretch their creases up black rock and roll leathered alleys, streetlight buttons, strapless lanes, bustier bustling buses, hourglass rain circular ring roads, art is consolation for the act of doing it. The love, over time, honey baby you have for a thing is commensurate with the chance the artist took, in their heart, and if they weeded out the well-done things and left the heart. If it was a course they took did well on, you wish them well but you may not love it. And babies, it's so dark outside, this morning.

I am that little locket auctioned off, at a fair ceiling. I am that post-mortem you bought. I am resting peacefully, in your sight. I am the camera-worker, the photographist, the limnist, I wrote you with light.

The bras. Blue angel powder puff of night, letters to the dead returned with an answer from the postmarked coffin, art is the result of what you, in your dogged hours, away from it, to keep going. This: I powdered my little heart-doggie with a shocking blue muff. With a little silk hook. A little satin hookie for some little blue nookie and I took my hairy little heart out for a walk. And Mark Rothko said, and Daddy RedRot said, and the Big Limnsters said, 'La tragédie, l'extase, le destin.' And Big Red said, 'La tragedia, l'extasis, el destino.' And I am feeling that blue and green with white feeling when I hear him saying again to me, tragedy, ecstasy, destiny. This is what I hear when the black night shines blue like a lady in a long red sheen. When paint, blues, paint, rock, pain, jazz, and photographs of old cigarette and booze ads 100 years old thrilled us, there were humans who wanted the conversation between art and the world to. Baby, I am lonely just like you. Let's talk. Let's be coffee brothers. Let's be espress sisters. Let us be in that daily waking up. Good morning babies. I am what comes with you in the bed before you even woke. So let me spin a little spoke, and you just dream on. You go back right into that good and you know you just had there a moment sentence. Just that curve just that note, just that shape, that locale, that point, that sense of the volume the air, the three-dimensional music of it you could ————————— feel just stops come. Just rest stops in the desert. Just ——— dog day desert dug an oasis. Just like that blue haze where it should take a breather of water, where be in the loneliness, again. I have walked my lonely heart out on a leash, without embarrassment. I was past embarrassment, and past shame. I was into Ben Webster on the just-before he blows that embouchure. I was in the embouchure of love of paint. I was where indigo meets the moment. I was with you. I was, with you. Let me hold you in my arms, by my words.

Mercy. And you know I talked myself into it, Frog and Hawk with a little post 'Friskin' the Frog' 'Blues for Yolanda' just for that Bill Holden that entrance just one summer-ni-i-i-i-i–g-gh's beat speed hip dip feeling the seconds before .. .. well that first snap pre little kimnovakian dog paddles to lust, don't you ever dream, again, of peace being more like Bill Holden you at night, so romantic. Peace is not kept by the bureaucracy. Mandarin mainstreams make art feel like world under barely suppressed ironic tyrants. Stay, keep those feet wet in other stay out of that mainstream, it is polluted, baby, come back to Love Street.

With killing invisible ironies, oh but when they bite it can be fatal, like one of them viruses, to your heart they say you do not rest from it, or else, along the lines of. Little heart jots remember a lifetime. Scribbling my way to you, drawing shapes here to make you like it, crawling alone the ground pushing a my little pencil, making pretty radio. Some nights, I swear I have seen the zenith of day. And Bill's holding you close in that kind of Kevin Spacey air, of 'What's Going On', oh but my, how you like it. The Boogie-Woogie Black Night. Anchoress Ave.

Just toking – me some Datura dated last night date-due asthma anodyne nigh well inhaled – well, tell me pace pain it'll fain dain a fandango down to me, Lord let it rain! I been coughing up that dog since I been your WAKE UP TOUPEES! DRIP THAT SURPLE DOWN!

Lay back on that heavenly snooze alarm, and grab yourself another life or two while you're at it, from that Great Smoke

Machine in the sky. Doctor Sky, please give me a little prognosis as to my scoliosis'll act up today if it don't rain. What's that? I think I see the Desert Fathers heading out for the 4th century. Just rain me. Rain me some T's on down. Always surprises. It's not what you like. It's not what you dream. Nor what you dream ——— : it's what you desire so, so that you keep at it, and it's not even that. It's what you do, and who you are, and how you love, in between all those times you can see, it's what you do you can't see keeps you going. It's not what you do. It's what you do when you can't do what you do keeps you going, is the unapparent thing apparent to heart, in its music. Poison skirts just to thrill you. With some one lift of a caught heart-pulled .. .. .. by (not to mention other places of old yore Childe Weenie days, run free at last) marlin monrowy billow skirt all upside down sidewalk vents, and loving. Like white stairs on a blue night, I have walked up the A-bomb emptiness to you, in the desert. I have been a red anatomical heart on a white stair-case. I have seen Death Valley make the sky black mountain peak hangings, and the earth all pink rising pink sky, at dusk. I am a dog for dusk. Dayenu Dog.

Sometimes when I got too sad I used to listen to the radio, for company.

And think of late August when the President's birthday ... ... came and got to dreaming of Algiers, and the River It is water which defines us. Water and lake, boy and man, lake and river, man and boy. .. .. That soft rolling like mountain plains. And when moraine again became mountains there's this sense: Even today it does not seem, some days, to have changed, so much. We still can't name it.

.. .. In the shadows we are all the same in the gloaming.

.. .. .. On a high long desert rock rock yourself in that big sky cradle. If we could name the desire, why would we collect it? And lest we forget to forego, we find we already done that.

We so to call up love, in the morning, sleepy, just to hear the same thing repeated, as once we imagined it.

6 seconds is plenty. 6 seconds is the world. I can tell you in 6 seconds, 'I never knew how much I would be thinking about you, all the time, all the years, before, but now it seems the way it is with my heart, thinking about you.' Okay. You're right. 7. – 7 seconds, took. Time is love. Time is this most incarnate thing we celebrate. OH BUT UGLY! Yever pick up a book, get it home, baby that white space got bad breath. Freshen up your whites, hon. Then your black shapes will follow suit most admirably, bark! Bark, you damn white space! Wake up! Git! Git! Sit! Stay! Sing! Why will those gutters not yodel? I ask you.

And in the sweet look of rain, in the morning.

I was always looking for them rain-slicked love-clicked kind of Atgety in the morning when the rest of us are asleep and he took the chairs asleep and took them while they slept and took the chairs' souls, their sole intention in looking so sexy. I myself have been a chair in various European locales, with a chair fellow as my comrade. Compañero Chairo, and the lutta did, baby, most swell continua and I woke to find my chest was a camera. I have carried the exquisite corpses of love's dropping in all my carry-on love bags, the world.

I have thought about you more than I ever could have imagined. When I smell White Ginger, you come back. When the stars crawl up the rose wall vineyards I have thought of you, a lot. When the corona and stigma and style of the passion opens, and dies, it is you, but I never told you.

Do you know?

Did you know?

This is Mercy coming atchoo. A little sound of a pic. Oh to only diddle is it Blues is, or is it Blues are, are Blues an is or are Blues an are, or is it Blues are not, or Blues is not, or Blues ain't. I loved the conversation between art and the world to – Baby I am lonely just like you. This is Miss Mercy on Lonely Avenue. Hey, and why not Avenue to Street. We could turn that Lonely

Avenue into Lonely Street and see how Lonely Avenue plays with two less beats. And Miss Mercy, would I be your Sister. (I have heard myself called Sister by men, in the night. Calling me Sister Mercy just a way may I say enlong – and this may be their way, the south. It may be how a tongues just elongate things just a bit, not *too* much mind, but kind of soften and stretch it a little bit, and maybe that is just the way I like that architectural call it tectonic look. I love the look of a long syllabic saliva to come just riding there on the page.

That sweet heavenly tongue gate.

Honey, I am your desert rest oasis rest stop, oasis. Walk me into the: ——— *haze!*

I'm looking for a little optical buzz.

I want to go into where dogs have disappeared, agog, into a fog, doffing fur underwear, and overcoats, in the rain supposing. I want to be the reed for heaven's mouth. I want the sky to blow. I want the sky to be packing rain, and I want to get into that little carry-on cloud accumulation bag, and I want to be packed with rain, by God. I want to be an earth saxophone for God's breath. I am stuck in this prison. I am bound in this cell. I am mercy in the mirror. I am bond to not being able to play. I play no instrument. I have no gift. I have unrequited love, for many things, and one of them is: sax. Oh to be a saxophonist now, in the dark night. Let me blow you what the President has blown me, by my words. I would like to much to do that. Right here, on this radio. Let the radio blow! Oyoyoy, let me be an oith saxophone. Looooooooove Street. Loooooooooooooonely St.

Where embouchures are sailing, baby, you will find me. Where the lips of the River Miss meet the moment of indigo's forming, I believe I will be in that number of reeds. And rushes? I do not mind. Let me be your rush hour, sleep. Here now in the loneliest time when those sleep switchbacks seem to be so circadian in their twistbacks you could flying off that sleep cliff down those stairways into nowhere, walking that car feet .. ..

.. .. I am thinking so often these days of *Last Tango in Paris* ... ... you know, you get into the real estate section, you get to a dream ... ... did I kill myself last night? You know I can't remember. I think I did, but I'm not sure. I been asleep picking up the phone, ZZZZZZZZ

Then I put my vinyl in my suitcase, now I am turntabling for you, I might have hung myself I'll take a look while this spins, and see I might've got hung up in that ceiling fan and hung. Did I ever tell you about the best muff I ever tasted down Central Grocery? Man, I am tasting that olive salad in my mouth right now. Maybe that was my last request. Maybe I died with the words 'Central Grocery ...' on my lips. I swear I taste a little olive drippings there, now. I don't feel too bad, you know. The shingles don't seem to be bothering me so much. I mean, deroofing. I mean – I mean, re-roofing. I mean where do you look, in the book to phone, SHINGLES – SEE ASS.

I been begging. You need a man come over.

I been pleading. To recover your ass parts.

Upholster my sweet settee. Sister Shingles, here. *Do* you call? Some sweet painful disgusting UG – LEE shingled ass I got here.

I will be spelled heaven by time.

I will date heaven, in the sea.

Baby expire on me. Do not be like me. Oh, but maybe you are. Just a little bit? Just a little bit bad? Just a little bit bad for me, as me thee? I have played *Last Tango in Paris*, with a soundtrack of James Booker. 'Black Night' did suffice. But then I really got dark. Dark, down. Dirty down and. Down and dirty and dark and put on 'On the Sunny Side of the Street'. And #2 thing is you know what? I might've. How would I know? This is New Orleans in August. How could I verify, am I dead or alive?

Any callers? Any clues? In the nightshoes, nightzounds, salt nighs and why not say, radio waves

Sweep Street. Elmore James Avenue.

Oh, baby, oh Lord. Baby. Days you wake up bed's up before you.

Bed's supped you're still asnooze dead. I think I'd like some time off from the coffin.

I feel like a body part on a stoop. Remember that lasttangoinparisy golden and blue winter rain in Paris. This is La Paix. Rooftops. I have longed for a man like my illicit love, who could be husbanding.

Me – know me that well how I'd be a skell, kill for looks of fish rooftops.

That rainy leather of Blue Slumograph breath.

Be a blues guitarist, a pencil reed harpist.

Word work is knowing heart from mind.

The easement accurate to emotion.

You can't look up heart.

Heart can't be looked up.

You can't look up your own one heart.

You can't.

#1 Rule of Life.

You cannot. You can't look up your own emotion. It's in your forearms.

Someone who has truly survived seeing?

Does not quite so easily, quite so beautifully.

They are much much more a Rosie Perez, a Jeff Bridges, in *Fearless*. They are much much less confident, and so in an appealing modest way.

Though content in a way I can't say.

It is something in the neighbourhood of ecstasy I speak about.

Though it can't be named.

It is as elusive as White Ginger. I have tried to draw this name. In the fold, the crease, the hang.

It may be the Soul's White Ginger.

If you love blues, the blues will sustain you. And if you love jazz, the blues will sustain you. And if you love blues the jazz is true.

It already jazzed you.

Let me be Big Red Rain. Let me be Miss Rain. Let be *A Nap Coltrane*. Let me coltrane you to yourself. Coltranearse. Let me be Mistress of Yore Rainy Day Water.

Let me be that first open crack of the wind.   When the door blows 'Stormy Weather', in the.

Rain which. Like a strong sense of falling in White Ginger makes me cream that: For hearts have lives of their own and live apart from us. Honey, I am living inside you. This is Mother Calamus Good Morning. Oh Momma you been hiding all that, and you know what baby, you are right. Though you sensed me and my vowels. I know. That love would find a way. Love, back in its room, baby, let me be that lost shoe. Let me just drop, sometime. Let my slide be what you slip your little art foot into, after the plenary has gone. Let me be that silver mule of Death Valley in the shining white salt sun. Let me a mule mirage, to you. Let me be a stiletto sun. Let me knife you. Let me be a dagger to the heart. This is your Mother. I been needing that ocean ozone, to sex me. I been needing to get down below, in the level of salt. I been needing to feel like a nitch blown up into blue ganglion weather. I been needing you. I been lonely late at night, like 4 o'clock in the afternoon. When James Booker was the Saint of Night. And I'm going to tell you a story. And it came to this. In love delta bars with record player rain suitcases. Tall hivers. Zoot l'hivers. Jerryrigged of organs, in bedscretions, joy in the moments; curs bring me Joy. Drinking up at CHARON's. The 441. Mezz. Malika. Midtown. And the unnamed ivy uvulations do not speak, they just undulated by benches, mutely. And if I plead to have loved you too much, books, then at least let it be love. And if I loved you, Radio, let it have been love, most Houndly. If you name me as ill, for my loneliness, what will you do it was only loneliness? And will you know the ill, if everyone is sick? And why do the helping professions change their names for things, so often, so seeming to civilians to be embarrassed by the emotion evoked by the very name of the very thing they treat? And why do decorators tend to call things, like artists, by the sturdy antic antique names of old? Maybe we should be interior decorating our loneliness; for then, the professionals would name the old names which had weathered all the crisis. And when the furniture of my intestine is carried about, let it at least be love of the arrangement. I want to show you the architecture of my heart, and use the plain or fancy words which hit my fit. Turn off the light, baby, and be in that single solo studio tango, for one. Baby do not fear me. I am you, inside. We are in this together. After all, we love the street, and we are not afraid of going outside into the big world of lane grease and alley shmutzerama-aroonie, I love you, darling, of that I am sure. I love you. I want you to know that. I love you. I do. I loved you, and I left you. I loved you in my dreams. I wanted you to come to me, by post, by mail, by phone, and say, Baby I can't live without you, live with me. Like a Lordy, Lady, I expected things to come to me. I was wrong. In the end, we are Gene Hackman in our underwear, our skin, in a lonely room, alone, with a chair and saxophone, way beyond sex desires, just tearing the wallpaper off the walls for who is after us, who knows what the walls say. In these effleurages of rage we have all been prone to, peeling off regret upon regret. Glorious and furious even if uxorious in bedrooms both slum and luxe lujo-urious curious as to what they will say, after we're gone. We have all been lit by Vittorio Storaro, we are all searching for that perfect appartement du tango. I have oft gestured in the night with one pale Conté. My fingers have Asthma Lights nicotine stains. I have, once in a while, smoked poison Datura. Which will help the asthma, also perhaps kill you dead. Having asthma is like being on narcotics, all the time. Perhaps there will, one day, be a holy War on Asthma, since, just by being, asthmatics have that ecstasy of not breathing, nearly all the while. They went after the Jews and they went after the blues and they went after the news. Only the wise knew enough to advise us, With some people it's always something. Flesh, chairs, carne, the dazed, amazed, crazed supposings. I have loved you so long. I have always been in an extreme state of looking. I have long longed for those allures were no-cures. I can't help myself. Let me bring you the architecture of Snoozeland. I can swing both ways. I swing over the border, I do not resist myself. Zed is as me to Zee, Zee as Bed-Zed, tell me. I can swing with a 44 as well as a horse-latitude 30. A man who tightens his e on every every, is as to me as a man who lengthens his every e. I have travelled far, in bed, to a right as a chirp, as I have to a right as a Barry White. Love haze as daze. Doze abecedarioly.

Z is a Z to me. I provide no pronunciation guide, I'm easy. Easy is right, easy is good, ease down, baby, to forget the going, with me. Go that way. I have lapped long southern z z z z z z z z z creamies, as I have lapped the heds of northern z z z z z z z z z s, of the dailies. I have known ems, I have seen ens, I have laid awake like a stone preoccupied, with leading. I have lain over and slept under an armpit so triggery, and woke knowing the answer to point size, I have seen the point of it all when a sweet goy boy toy has been pointing to heaven. Sagrada Familia, Gaudi, I do say! When it comes to love letters I am an andro-gezederzee. I am vittoriostoraroly cinesinamatographicoemotio – nally ——————————— thee. I peeped out of flies Z as Z. They seemed to pee in bed more or less the same as me. Z met Z in sleep and seemed to be bliss, mixed. I provide no proper introduction. This is magic. Baby, come with me. I provide no expert witness line-up, for my own defence.

I do not explain myself, I love you.

Since this is not science, I do not have to prove anything. I conform to love, no other. I provide no extroduction, no back-door intro, magic alone.

Come with me. My hands are above the table, at all times. Come into time with me. This is time, shaped. This is the architecture of my heart. Come into it.

I am feeling parched. I remember Death Valley. I could be salt. I could be a little lick waiting for some. The air's so airless it could be a lame hairless, tell me. Ah, the Devil's Golf Course.

I believe I see the parching haze. I believe I can feel that cine salt desire, returning. Let me be your cine escort. Let me be your desert aisle companion. That voice in the dark, lonely, of a day you'd know with your eyes closed in a red plush worn.

Oh, sleep. Ever know how so many of your favourites are the ones you can't remember if you saw it. Now there is a mystery of the universe. The shows you have to go back and get out, because you can't remember if you saw it, in some certain feeling of remembering makes you love that strange feeling it gives you, to not know. That's movies.

– Is it Sunday.

– It feels like Sunday. DUST MY SWEET STONE.

– I'm feeling lonely. DUST MY BLUE PONTOON.

POSRAIN.

POSWAR.

POSLOVE.

– Papers on the bed.

– Slept the Real Estate.

– Used my STYLE pillow / ARTS down.

– Plague did not betray me / You did.

spread your love around –

– I'm The Glamourama Hound

– Among Us   Sweet Grammour Skin Of Us

          Dust

– The Arthritic Angelic

with *The Anchoress*

Night Heart
This is the heart of night here with you
You got brooms I'll dust your brooms you got moons I'll dust
your Junes-prunes! Baby I'll dust you up your regulation-
prunes baby you got some radiant radiation prunolas I'm ready
with my little duster fly. I'll do you a Drive-By dusting Honey
you looking for dust.
　　See in the paper today?....
　　You got cornflakes?
　　You got a can of corn Corn of corn, you got an easy pop fly? /
You got yogurt, got some culture baby. Some en-zyme needs
dusting off. In your fulltime no or on and off on guy – This is
radio for the blind.
　　We are all blind.
　　In love at night.
　　In the dark with our eyes
　　closed on the radio pillow
　　we can see so sharp.
　　Hey baby you sighted – sighted or
　　blind from birth suddenly
　　woke up blind or you
　　fully sighted baby you a　　sighted soul – I'm going to sweet
talk
　　you down so bad
　　you'll be seeing the best pictures of all. Those
　　　　　　　　　　　　　　　　　　These
　　ear pictures.
　　These pictures woids are you,
　　those pictures words can give you
　　baby and this
　　I believe
　　you already most surely know.
　　I believe
　　you know what

I look like.

You don't need eyes for that.

You just use your head.

Ain't radio so – visual baby – Oh man

nothing like the blues is re. So keep those eyes   there right there in the middle of your head Honey   keep those nice good pictures – alive.

This is Mother Mercury

Let's have some of them fine radio ——————————*fu-u-u-u-u-u-u-u-u-mes.*

It feels like.

What number does it feel? Let the

Wake up, body parts!

Get those dismemberments a move on!

Get some chocolate pain on the go. Let the

Get a half-moon moving.

Get a honeymoon to moon your luna de miel. Me? I'll fill my cornice with honey.

Me? I'd be glad to just, well. Let the. Let Lethe rivers rain. Let your soul be blue with rain. Let Lethe rivers run. Let the red rot net be your blood and let it fall. Don't you love how blood is 3 standey-talleys and two oo's.

Like 2 tall buildings and two headlights and a headlight parked. I so love ink.

Alive with lu-u-u-u-u-u-vvvve. A-live with duuuuuuuuuuu-uuuuug daaay–dust. Dig them dug day doggies high. Dig them dog day dugs, you got dust you want me to dig baby, I'm there. Baby you got flakes 'n' milk's needful of dusting, hey put me on the redial. Put me on that energizing dust, put me on escort dust, put me on longneck dusting buster, baby you got a long-neck needs dusting-by Daddy? You got Daddy Dust there on your preferred band numero uno button on your Daddy Machine, hope so. How's abouts some ——

Around about now – .

– Dust up them pictures in your head.

With some Sinatra here – radio to radio.

I have been mounting the stairs of love.

Before that. And before that. Before was.

And before that. First up: was Sam Cooke. And would a Camel hold my clothes? One hum.

A little hump? A small Came? A craven drag?

A desert orange? A gold? An old gold? Ochre?

A sailor? A player? A rot? A lucky sunstruck?

Craving some walking. With you. In dark velvet.

Oh, my toes are doing a Sinatran fungus scat.

Them toe mushrooms are singing some doobeerots.

Fungoid DOOBEE-2BS, piggymarket *Whap do whap*s.

Mercy. I'M MY RAG! The lineup Pharoah Sanders from the album tribute to Coltrane. If you're driving thanks for the lift. Thanks for welcoming me into your living room front seat. Or may be dining as we while. Idling your chomp in your bedroom dash. After the music began. Abraham I been thinking about you, baby. Give me a call. You lying, you just woke up. You were saying previously Hey somebody come here with that mallet, what? Somebody please, come malletize me. And they did. Now you woke up, you're lying there like some kind of type paralysed state. Huh. Yeah. Like some kind of state you got lung borders baby. You're just lying there viable ain't ya. Yeah, well now you just go on back to sleep, here's something superduper on the decaf side'll send you back (there was a cut of something I'm thinking of a guy sitting on a cloud – oh something about bananas and rain, and the way those I don't know – banana leaves sway, close-up.) Don't you love those little flashes, baby.

Don't you love those little flashes baby, when the room's getting so dark, don't you love how dark it is. It could be the first dark by the the light of a smoky morning it's so dark. It could be the first colourless lightning of a rainy lightning day, it's so dark. Check out those arms and shoulders of those banana leaves baby. Do you not – whoo – one more flash – don't you love the lightning and thunder show – Night.

– Can't you wait to get your parched bird beak up to that sky. Come on down Mr Sky – it's dry down here. I was in bed. Now I'm with the door open. Taint.

I been thinking you a long time, Saint Sweet.

We rode up the gold cab on the grid. Girdle.

Mr W was peeping out of that non-existent 13. At me and Saint Sweet. Love was lobbying little peeks.

We was doing things. You been that place.

Put Marvin Gaye in the great Saint Coltrane.

Art is what you do to finish it. Love is what you do to finish, in the making. Starting anything is not love. Though it may be an affair. It may not even be an affair. It may be a complete misunderstanding. Let me be your little Customs Officer of Love. Pleasure is my business. I am no volunteer hanging around a street corner, saying:

'Don't pay me for lovework, throw me 50 bucks for a year's work.' Not me. Bluefinger worker, me.

Me? I am doing lovework for money.

Honey love me. Come elevator fever me.

I been making mercury mirrors, for you.

Just for you, love me. It was the romance of those who did not do artwork, themselves, that the arts including writing was romantic done by volunteer whores. When real artists know it like being in sales.

Sales in love, of love, of love's offproduct, worked, in means, for means and means and means and only means knowing ideas may diddle but only in the found means does it become a product, the genteel like to dream of artists as dogs only blueskying.

But in means meant much more intimate, to intimate love, with every syllable. Saint Sweet otherwise known as Johnny

Coma in civilian life on Civvie Street my post-mortem soldier.

I daguerreotyped him in old back in the days.

Times Square Hotel, I made a mirror of mercury of the corpse by flashing neon.

It was a beautiful thing, to love a guy. It was beautiful. It was. My romance. We rode up the elevator of love, this modern intimacy.

We rode the gold tomb. Strangers in a mirrored Poe nightmare, got sweet.

Strangers when the two arrows pointed to each other, friends after the affair when the arrows parted back to back.

In two minutes of an instant we stopped on non-existe treizième. We have still not, humans in the cities, gotten used to the weirdness, elevators.

It's like going to movies.

The fast vertical's the dark. His name was Johnny Coma, and he daguerreotyped me. He mirrored my soul. He *did* capture my soul: the idea – this's why.

Johnny Front, Johnn Coma, Saint Sweet.

He stole my soul. Why else? To make the thing the heart remembers, alive. I died in open-heart surgery and he fumed me, ride up. I been working with this mercury so long and have also come through the yellow all right. Did I die of yellow? Did I die of Jack? Lord, why are we here? Are we even here at all? Is this a dream of the dead? Am I what God does, diddling?

Love God, and hang, paraphrasing the Saint. Are we God's hang? Are we what God does, other than love us. What is this thing called pride? This sin. Even if it skell-aliases itself today as self-esteem.

To think better of yourself – didn't we use to call that totally conceited?

We are taking courses in becoming totally conceited, and so smiles the state. The poor, the dispossessed the ruddy coat-brown coatbound heat –

– have been removed, while we jollied our good feelings about ourself and circulated a brochure advertising our lack of love charity. Sugarless.

You don't have to feel good to give. You give. It's an act. How you feel doesn't come into it. That's the curse of THIMNKS.

Let me be your geek. I have loved you like a pickle.

Lush life. Rain. Nudies. Blues. Sax. Jazz. Lonely Avenue. Lonely Street. Lonely, Love, Last. St.

I have been a miracle gherkin, for thee.

I have been a simple blind Datura Tree. I have met you, before. I'm not sure what age.

I may have been your noose, your frail. I have walked around wearing myself as a wall.

And pinned a heart on me and it was not symbolic.

It represented itself.

It was its own proxy, love.

It had its own life, it breathed, a heart.

A heart with lungs. These are the ways we make music. To have a heart like a diaphragm. I have long given my love to Lester Young, so he might make it dead even sweeter than alive, for me. And sometimes, some days. Some days, this did transpire. In Vietnam days, I loved a soldier. Let me hang with you as the many Datura skirt nooses. Let me your noose and frail as a gumshoe's moll of purchase. Speculate I am the music you heard as you walked along you sensed was behind you. I was. Let the X Let the Let Lethe rivers rain. Let your soul be blue with rain. Let the red rot net be your blood and let it rain. Love is not something you think about, love is something you do. The day you were born, you were able to. Some chose not to, having the option. I put myself in the doghouse for you. I was your little schnauzer seductor. Your retriever of lovewoid. Your collie of word collars. I was a skell for literature. I wanted to commit the crime of ink. I wanted to be love's fink. I wanted to be a rat stoolie for love. Of love. I wanted to tell all, on love.

| 73

(Remember Goldblum in *La Mouche?* Ah, don't you love how temptation turns tent?)

I wanted to tell

it for

you. I wanted to

be a prisoner. I am.

I can't help it, babe.

I'm a fly on love's wall.

(a dog

fly)

And Marvin Gaye was on the radio. And Marvin Gaye sang, 'Mercy Mercy Mercy, the Ecology'. Long ago during Vietnam. (See: *Midnight Cowboy*. That feeling. Same as today.) Our souls far off like dots on Poverty Common. I was who you knew, once, in a plastic wrap.

How long? A lifetime, I say, plus three seconds. As long as a Sinatra 'terri*ffffffff*ically', God bless.

I may have hung last night.

It's so hot who knows?

Do I smell? Give me a call. You want to watch some TV together? Call me up. It's the dark part of Miró which gives us joy. The man is just a gesturing pessimist he just makes every orifice of this necrosis don't know aboutchoo (Gesundheit. Zie gesund.) joy.

And Marvin was my song.

And 'St Sweet' was on the radio and Saint Sweet came into the elevator, he was a vision of raindrops. This in a time my Husband Number Never-Mind?

Got in bed with me you ever have those days, babes you feel like, to him, you're his member of the general public and the public, in general's been told your private nicks. You're like La Peste de Nookie. Saint Sweet? I was right up his alley, one time, in some sweet leather supposings. I was his little rain bonnet. He just folded me up to carry with. Just be a little rêve protect.

A condom du dream. (Du cream.)

I been listening to that 'I Been Working' off that here's a little 'I Been Working' off that *A Night in San Francisco* album off
of you gotta love Van – he was our poet when poets became
embarrassed of the heartfeltednesses, of it all, and went *on* to
novels, and wrote them without any poetry; saying. I have been
a moil at hurricane brises. I have been in a hurricane brassiere
suddenly turned into a brasserie à deux more like some of them
brass afternoon ho's been a hose and a creamsplit, dancing.
And now after that 'I've Been' ((not an 'I been,' –)) '– Working', let's move on down to a little and you know it's true. I
always do. Forget to remember I always forget: 'I Forgot That
Love Existed,' but when I hear it, I love it. Like that B.B. thrill
which is always so good to hear, gone. From the word go went
and went from go to gone, and yes I have, Lord. I have been
roiled by world, moiled like wild hurricane brises. A Night in
Saint Francis, I have felt it. From the angels, too. From The
Meadows, also. What is exotic to *your* heart is all that matters.
Matter excitations have been to me greater Metropolitan Blues
of one syllable, off another latitude. Woild, and raht, could last
me a lifetime, of love, in the ear so aural so sex like than anything, ships loosened their stays and the sea came in over the
city and all cities are Venice, in love, ain't they? Oh baby. And
the seas of the rivers of the lower quarters of love, just lowered
themselves for love. His little daily bread basket canasta of
sweet care, plopped. His little alley lovestove, his little sweet
roll tumbled for him in turn. And the night made pre-hurricane
lightning. And the night came down like thunder pilings. And
pilings were broken levees of love, and the the floods came.
Crosses flew off Cathedrals and it was too operatic for words
like chance Pharmacia *La Bohème* making of all rooves old
blue feathered Paris. And little dormers caught at corners, at
just such an angle that yellow you never much favoured looks a
pale you love, all of sudden spotted at the corner of Saint Anne

or was that Street Saint Peter and is that Ann eless or e — .?
Chancing to take the time to look, broken by heat. Just moving
rather tortoise-like, so far behind the times, you become ahead
of the times, unembarrassed, because love makes you, to just
be where you are. Not born out of time, out of sync, but just
right as you, in means, all of sudden, suddenly you least expect
it. Oh. Oh about say somewheres between ten after 4 and say
maybe 12 after 5 on some heartstuck afternoon when all of sudden that sky goes away and rain replace it. It is the hour right
now gets 3 3 1/2 hours before sunset or do I mean 2 when white
pages like this are I'm working on are pink and the blank is a
pink wall and not a white one and pages have been bounced
pink off of red walls and certain sky curtains, out there. And
the sky's blowing Ben Webster, and that river water is sailing
the President of Love right to left across your eyes above the
sidewalk way down Ursulines and like a heart president it does
present itself, love, in the meantime you never expected to be
soon. Nor I. No, nor normally as to say like Big old rust barna-
cles float like Torah ships and love the silver pointer and like a
righteous blue gourmet barnacle, Lester Young blew us. I have
lived through names. Not in any tongue you know but only in
that lovetongue molecules. Like any mole in a heat suppose you
are just wandering, that sweet. Thou Swell. Saint Sweet one
night was just that sweet supposing. But his body was lit from
way back in the lobby. I have been in most optimistic dark hour
— like a petitioner to the court, the Court of the Court of
'They', afraid to be a courtesan of art, baby, flirt for pay world.

And when I saw Saint Sweet, baby? And when I saw Saint
Sweet? When I saw Saint Sweet my heart knew how it had been
lying. Things, people, books, a pic, a painting, a store closes, an
odd comment — your heart recognizes its lies. Eyes, direct.
You're up in the dark part, knowing, of Saint Sweet Street. Doc
Holler. The Doctor of Love Is In. La Doctora. (*Doktor!*) The
Professor of Your Heart. Profesora Heat. La Doktora de

Humiditia. Tu Tia de Auntie Histamine is down making her yellow curly lugs. Oh, the fever. I have had yellow, I have come back. Do I have malaria? How do I look? Do I look fat? Contest: how many chins? Do I have enough chins to be a radio? Ladies, let me tell you, gents, reptiles and lizards, longjohns and shortshorts, this is the kind of man I have always found was being my potential of fancy: He kept me a secret.

He kept beeswax separate from business. I was that little gold heart he wanted to wear. To pin, later to some miracle wall, to hope. No symbols, only looking. Later he'd pin me, in public, where others gave thanks. And they would know. Art knows. Art tells the story. Art, in company, tells the crime. Out on good behaviour before you begin? Think again. What I said stood for naught. He knew it. The thing itself. The thing. The thing. The thing. He was a man of occasion who liked. Yeah. Just cross the river, see how Charon's doing. Getting on. Check the book on the pennies. And I'll tell. I'll tell you, further what kind of guy's my fancy man. Who likes just: To occasionally just hang around in the great inconsequentials which make up the civilized world. Oh aught. You little naughty bagel hole. Habits? I've had many. I was a human. Prudent? Rarely. I was a child of my times. Fear? You bet. I shot from high buildings with vertigo, I went to war zones scared of blood, I went into the dark because it thrilled me, I have a scotophilic soul. My need to have God watch me was greater than any fear I knew. What dark alley compares with Yom Kippur? What war zone compares with the blue coming down, just so, before that first star lights in October come World Series time and I have enjoyed more than any sex act that illicit pastrami, again. And I have waited paralysed to be a word on the cutting room floor. A red cut of God's Final Last Rewrite. I believe God could be anything, what if God is not female? Do I care? What if God dresses as Judy Garland? Big Time Girl Sailor Boy Hello! Relax Chicas Necro How Hung Heaven Sale Burrito Hale I Live At

Love And Lonely On the: Oh to be funked, in summer: All God's children got chicken necks, Nola: Going down the gorgle wattles on the funk. On the one in the funked-up garden gorgleizing. Les Blues. Los Blues. Die Blues. Blue Avenue. Rue Bleue. Avenida Azul. Down the low limo horizon. Out on the red shimmer highway. Slow down them wattles, slow your drag down. Slow down your gorgle metronome. In a green gazue ragland.

Should I give a damn? I don't. I do not. If God wants to go around as Marilyn, why should it bother me? it does not. If God wants to vamp Gilda in some tubshow why do I bother, I do not. It is such a very short life. Why not leave God alone. He made Lester Young. Is that not enough for our little night neon kvetches of illumination? He made Van the Man. Is that not enough to make us kvell some sweet harmonious neon? He made Ben and Miles and Bird and Presidents and Vice-Preses and the diddle between to dither to no of a Pres or a Prez, is this not dayenus sufficient? He made Junior Wells. Why would we not give thanks, for it? He made Buddy Guy, he made Junior, he made Jimmy Witherspoon, is a 'Spoon not sufficient? He made Charlie Musselwhite and Charlie Parker and *Charlie Varrick* and St Charles Avenue and streetcars inaccurately referred to as trolleys. Why is that not enough for a snit on a Saturday Night as well as those venom wrong-the's excuse me. He made Bobby 'Blue' Bland and Bobby Blue Bland and Bobby *Blue* Bland, is that not enough difference? He made Joan Manuel Serrat and Saint Joan and St John of the Cross, why do we need a reason to hang ourself? Is not life reason sufficient? I will miss you, too. I know. It's just the way it is. There is no reason. Don't look for, one. I have loved, I have lost, I am no special thing. I am you. That it is. It just – is. It is just – love. Is it not enough that in my darkest hours what kept me from going off the end was Percy Mayfield. If I had not had 'Life Is Suicide' to be followed by 'Underlying Depression' as a chaser I would have jumped off the fan illumination onto the fleabed, long ago. And past. I had a habit of falling love with men, in hotel rooms. Them wee wee hours of the morning. And let it be. And just a. Glamourous by La Mer. El Mar. I need some sharp shadows of the black and white outside. I need world to glamourama hound me. Making art has much to do with being a peeping dick in a lobby, an alter

Lord .. ..
(Mercy Street)
Broadcasting my love to you in the dark a.m.
For who did be a word ship in the
For who did dig the scary and yes it is and meant so way the rhythm of life catches us so unawares, sometimes. What if that one you saw, so heartstruck was the one?
... There on Love Exchange and you never took the chance. Leave ME, rush out and find her. What if you met her, up north, 'nother time, 'nother place, never suspected, did not know it was her, she wore her hair so different, or the context fooled you. Or the lack of hearty, the too many people.

Missing the long long empty dead stage sense of a big proscenium to examine in the Dead Quarter Days, in which to examine her off at the distance getting closer all alone coming down towards the river, coming. Daze. Choose your pic. When days are daze, better run after her. You might know her voice. Just that word, that one sound, that one low-peeped syllable. Ears peeping you become good at, you need to, have to. I am very good at recognizing voices, sitting in lobbies long behind newspapers. Both reading and pretending reading. I have carried torches behind headlines. I saw you. I did.

I am thinking of you now. Let's buzz while. I am 100-plus kilometres of butter and joy. I am love, on the radio. I am direct. Live and direct.... ....

...

Didn't you? I loved to peep a book like a guy across a lobby, coming out of an elevator. Peeping the one I liked, walking away, keeping it in mind, pretending to gander the other. Keeping something in mind I didn't know what it was trailed after me, the bookstore. Then, was it me, or them? Those pretty longplay book curves got jumpy, jittery, scared, afraid too many words might be seen to be congregating, and for too long. All kind billystick asterisks wading in to keep order. Man, some days, some books, I'm, 'Honey that page's net's so close you're going to wake up, "Why's my do so flat?"'

I am heading down, baby, to the lowest rung. Come with me? I am heading down to the rungs of the ladder down below the sea level. Down with the fishes, oh so pretty in blue augustinian August august poverty. I am paying for many things I would do again, no doubts, there.

My romance? My romance, with the dark. My romance, with the cave of it all. Just noodling these — last wee hours, of it. Did I die?

How do I look? Do I look dead, to you?

I got a new lamé morgue gown on, I got my morgue slamé smashing mules, may I say.

Thinking about the nuns, once, who burned themselves, for peace. That love beyond our understanding. Who burned for peace, because peace was their lover. A love we took, so much, for granted. A love we did not believe. We marched for it, but we did not love it. We marched for it, we campaigned, we did not know. We brought in peacekeeping uses, but we did not know that it is not any of those political things, keeps love and peace alive. It is the thing, itself. We did not even know what love was: and we thought we could find out what is it. We did not even know that to love a thing that much, will forever, be a mystery. And we would not be that mysterious. We have so long, now, child. Children, I tell you. We have so long. For. For so long. We have, for so long now, presented art, with the evidence as to its love in advance. What greater thumb in the nose of love is there, than this. We replaced love with the ironic. True. Once, in a tub at the Columns, up St Charles, when everything was spring and about to die, I lay just in the crook of the back of the front of a guy I loved so very much. And it is not that it was tragic. It was not tragic. It is not. It's not to this day. I'm too much of a romantic realist. A romance materialist. It is the mystery of the material. The love, in a tub, and Ben Webster off on a little boom box, made three. Room 16, and I'm in room more apartment, more slave quarter top floor, hidden, now, here, these years later. I thought it would be appropriate to hang myself, where once it was love, and in celebration. I object to killing myself with the advice of ghouls, strangers. I object to ghouls who have no art to offer, picking my bones after, calling it biography. How could they know the heart of one, which one other, even in a bathtub in New Orleans, even long ago, the spring of the flood, even then. Even being in wars with him, even dying and being alive at the end of every morgue day ... ...

They are shut out, forever, from the love syllables.

They are not permitted in, to the love. Only the love transformed, or translated, only and ever.

If I were a topic, I would be in the library. If I were an insect I would be on a slide. If I were a stat find me under sociology. But I am a heart. A heart with a camera for a pen. A heart with a pen for a camera. If I needed to wear a geek, I would. If my geek wanted to gull it, would I argue with it? Lord, if my pickle were You how would I know you from Lordy!

And my pickle, Lordy, Lord wanted to play me the blues and were a pickle slum, how could I say no to it, if it made me pretty music? If my slum pickle wanted to ride some blue bubbly white United up uptown to Tip's and sit on a sax, could I refuse it? Would I? Could I? Just a little bit? A touch? I promise I won't do anything. If I were a fog thesis I could hire a fog T.A. to travel its assisting ass to go tell me what the normal seasonals were, by records but I am a fog watcher, an eye. A sky love. I married sky. Since then I have been, with humans, a human bigamist, of heart, with humans, married to sky. I was not a witness to war headlines, I was a witness to war. I have been an eye at the spot. I am an iris with music, and I goddamn fucking wish I could play the sax! Lester Young has said everything I strive for. Lester has said it all.

It is over, it is not worth it, it is all worth it, one man, one chair, one Alvin lost. We shipped our comrades in reporting home. Even then, even now, even then, in a tub so close having known things together, what did we know? Gornisht. It was love. And there is no knowing love. It is love, after all. It is God's mystery. It is as mysterious as the invention of the saxophone. Which may balm us in the palmy days, too. And if all we were brought here for, was to hear 'My Romance', done by Ben Webster, for four minutes and bump seconds, would that be so terrible. Would 'My Romance', 4: , only, be such a terrible thing. A life? Who knows? Who can say. Not I. I am here for something. What?

You tell me. I am here. I am now. I am everything I am, right here, right now, I regret absolutamente nothing. Rien.

Bigtime nadita. I have moved on from nothing, evolved to nothing, improved to nothing, gotten better at nothing, I was a seed, I grew. Is that not enough?

What is it, exactly we were looking for, except a romance with world?

I am back of the street, back of the gate, back of the patio, back of jasmine, back of the ginger, back of the jessamine. I am a thing going to the rotted pot of summer, the summer's rot pot pourri.

I will be a scent, maybe, left, to linger, a lingering or nothing at all, and truth? I do not mind.

I have had few successes, but so what? I am healthy. Missing a few feet here and there, but hey, so what, aren't we all. You may find my right foot in some Dotel Motel and if so, have fun with me, at least, in that one-bit mountain massage à la no room service cart but a certain off-the-beaten-motel kind of weirdness of a geek at peace, at least. No more. And if that 4 minutes should become 6, well then. Two more minutes before the plane goes is a lifetime, a life. And 30 extra seconds is what we have prayed for. 'You're hooked, you're cooked, you're caught

'in the tender trap.'

Is this extra not Sinatran, never mind Sin, big Caps or sin small, enough, to be lagniappe-y grateful.

For?

I ask you.

?

It may be the time for that one person to round the bed of the hospital floor, lost, before we die. If all we had, in surplus, as little lost lagniappeys come home, were a trail of bread-crumb Ben Websters, in bed, with us, at last, would it be so dif-ficult, in fall.

In fall, in winter, in spring, in summer, would it? I think it would not be. Darling, I am in bed with you. Let me talk to you. Let me be. Be with me. I am on your pillow. Let me be your pillow. I will. And if it should be 7-plus minutes we must be grateful, for all. We are in the cave away, together. Just you and me. I am on Love Street. (I will hang by August's end.) I *am* where indigo meets the moment. I am of fog writ. I am Sky's Rag Peddler. I *am* the wife of sky. I am fog, ago awhile past. I am the horses of purple of the lower Quarter low gloam of hot late early twilight become the giant jasmine bugs growing and buzzing like wired pylon streetcars. In nice Carrolton swing and

on where the gins sing up St Charles down Canal a block, getting cool — easement off a.c. store blows making the street the room cooled to walk in go cuply, in through there down out of beyond uptown while I.

In the dark, hung, in taxis undressing, myself, and others, pleased. I am the ragpicker of moments. I am sky's collage. I have been exquisite, by night, in my dreams to the pieces of this and that pleased me. I wandered in and around the shape of words which *are* love objects. Words have always *been* photographs to me. They were my first lovelimn objects. I am. I *am* the embouchure of indigo.

I *am* the river's mouth. Lester Young has blown me in my darkest hour there will always be Lester. There will always be Pres.

There will always be rivers to cross.

I'm a Styx Stile fix, baby give me a call. Scratch me up. I am in the cave. I am a cross.

Between a ragamuffin and a rag and bone girl.

Dirt is not foreign to me. I'm a shmata. Ragsville. Way back. Over time. Over the years.

Those days them days, was. Past days times back before yonder shadow love.

The world tour of the genteel, today, is to help a lonely die.

Instead of Paris, afraid to be a tourist, introduce the Nozzle of Figaro, long-distance into a garage, oh but what clean hands! They started with the dead. To kill them.

But the dead wouldn't die. There was this shock of it's being one world and once you make a thing, it competes with the dead of ever, so the dead would not go away. So they began to kill off the living because the dead of art would not die.

I was born to be a dog, in a dogged family. Nip, nip, nip, at that rag. Soy la shmatte. Soy La Shmattita. You tell me. Mira la shmatte. Regardez moi la shmatte. Mi nombre es trapo. Rapo, pano, andupo, Lerapo Marx, call me Comrade Red rag. I belong to the red net – of night fish hose districts at the bottom of the sea. Means of blood murders. Catch them strobes, baby.

| 84

My God, God's hung. Check them towers of Gaudi.

In the dark like cabs all sung.

I been mailed mould, from above. I been mailed a little *pretty-eye*, a stranger, Burgundy, with the accent on the gun. It's strobing, it's Gaudi towering, out there, strobing, it's strobing, strobe strobe strobe strobe Morse code lightning flash flash flash strobe orange night strobe light light light strobe to death you get caught, I am in the black cave of night. This is the Negro Motherwell I have been seeking. I am in the dark night day is in Spain in France, in Spain north in France south in the day, I am in that black negrito Motherwell taught me.

I am in the negromotherwelliana of New Orleans. I am in my negroy blanco night. Not a goy in sight but only black night and all Nolaers Jewish to me, in a way. In a way I can't say but know to be true. True as a guy saying, 'Hey pretty eyes', mailing me some mould down by the rust above, the post office.

There's a stillness I can't explain. I have loved peace in my dreams. I have sucked peace off. I have creamed FOR peace. I have loved peace, most, in wartime. I came home and I saw such taking-for-granted, it seemed as if the cause of war, was suddenly apparent.

Peace is not genteel. Regimes are.

Peace is the street, noisy.

Regimes are dead quiet.

What is the name of taking things for granted?

The sky is ochre desire, waiting for thunder. (I will dig, 'I will dig you in the early bright', again, time and again, step up to 'I dig you', so dogged the changes wrung out the dog will rang.) The sky is vermilion in its million little light tickles, oh yes.

Consensus and art should be strangers.

Including everyone may be simply depression.

Baby! I have been dreaming of Jack Kerouac.

Baby your leather last night was as black as a Jack Kerouac

shadow. Take care of me.

Peace is kept by art. Love alms. Peace is not kept by calm. Peace is kept by hots. Peace is not kept by the well-done, behaved. Peace is kept by the naughty, private. Each one. Way we carry ourself, in this brief diaphragm. Peace is kept by music. Sax, sex, soul, funk, blues, R and B and or & B, both and jazz. Peacekeeping in the same committeetalk does not keep peace alive, it kills peace and keep the bureaucracy still sounding same old bureaucratic. Jack, you were my St Jean-de-Luz, de Paix. My Saint Jack of Night, de la Paz. Love. My Jean-Louis of St Louis Armstrong St I have seen house paint be the sky of negroy azul. I have seen the sky be the housepaint brush of ochre sunlight. I have yearned in a yen for certain latitudes. I've been born to crosshatch. It is not if you could do as well as X artist. It's not if you did do as well as Y artist. It's if you would be willing to go public for the rest of your life and forever with that. Standing in the shadows knowing you can is kind of psycho-y. It's like a mental disease. It's like jalousies. And jealousies. A different dark night. The paralysed kind. Love, I've been thinking about you a long time, now. I have carried you on my back like lyric luggage. I have carried you on my back like lyric lunchbox letdowns. I have carried you on my back like giggles up the lurch. I have lurched into lost left luggage depots and found you locked forever in the lockers not in use. I have lost you ten thousand times. I have found you in old *Lyric* shmutzhausen, Times Square, I have taken the PEEP-os before they were wrecked. Oh I loved PEEP-o neon. (I heard humans who had never *seen* Times Square happy it was cleaned up.

(Now their fear of New York City felt better. Like humans who felt better that the bars in the parts of town they would never be seen dead, were clean, now. There was an epidemic fear of world. ... ... [Humans who had a passing interest in words wanted to kill them.])

This is only another form of paint.

It's graphic art done by one heart artist.

This is paint, not ideas. Ink on rag. I have one bucket of white; I have one bucket of black. That is what this is. Black and white, no more, no less.

... Four oh two fifty.... Almost 4:03 in the a.m.

The Scripture of the Golden Eternity.

In my borderless heart have I loved you. You. Baby it was the touch of your 'Right', like raht. But spring was always rivers, pink blossom shuffles, rain which never ended like streetcars of mist. Life is a Hurricane of the great green light anticipation. The earth will not remember you. Nor will *Hymns To The Silence*, though you loved it.

The earth was not your lover. You loved the earth. But the earth did not love you. While you loved the earth, the humans you loved went away. Love of the earth is always unrequited. It is a rehearsal for God. I sat on Lonely Avenue, and said, 'Do I know you well enough to make you, née Avenue, now mine, Street?' But there is human love, this gift. I do not know where it came from. I saw words die. Many were pleased, by that. Many were pleased, at it. They did not love words, so they did not mind it. Just because words are our gift does not mean we know them, at all. Just because words are our gift does not mean we know them, at all, one bit. Just because words are our gift does not mean because someone says they love words, they mean it. They may not know what to love words, is. They may use words to say it, but they might as well be talking in paint. They may use words to say it, but they may all well be talking in aintz. Masters of words use their first tongue, as a second language. Some tried to write, using their first. Fine.

But you can't make whoopee using your first tongue.

The touch of your lips on my neck from behind I imagined when I saw your back down at the Le Croissant D'Or, for the first time, why, just yesterday. Baby, this is for you. This is for your 'Hi'.

Unless you come at it, through it, like longlost latelife love, found. The best you can do, using your first tongue *as* your first, in words, is the very-well-done. Sometimes it is as proud as a report card.

The clouds were as big as Heap City. Highrises of the Gods. Accumulated cumulus evidence, God's DNA.

The sky rose out of the river. Fish flew. The sky dried below in its very puddles. Rain deserted.

My soul. I packed a whack of rain, in my suitcase, and carried it on.

I kept rain like a bomb shelter supposed cans. I stayed underground like Lascaux rain, yet discovered.

I sat listening to the sounds, outside. Friends, walk with me a bit. My toes are sugared off.

I have vet feet. Diabetic, amped, blown off. Walk with me, into the desert. Walk with me, friend, love out into the far blue mountain desert. I have to tell you. The sound of a monotone? It is pornography to me. In the palmy days of love, porno monos to heart. Are we dead, already? What if we died? And what if this was heaven. Is?

And enough, in light.

Wouldn't we want heaven, to be pretty? Would we not want heaven to elide? Wouldn't we want elisions as pretty as *A Streetcar Named Desire*, now the bus?

(Whose genius as a title is not only the *Desire* no one else, quite like Tennessee, saw. But also that *Named*, versus a called). Would we not want to not change a bit of it, being as died?

What if we were dead, and forever, wouldn't you want to let vanity ride? We choose our breath. Humans sound exactly like what they intend to. Pity the apologist. They are explaining why flat is music. And you know it isn't. They play you for a fool, intend to, see what you do, and if nothing, play the shame for all it's worth in public. When flat words were said to be music, we said nothing. We saw it happening, and what did we do? We were so ashamed what had been done to words, we praised who had done it, so it wouldn't have happened. Not to us. Who loved our world, so. When the very thing most flesh which makes us us was being tortured and made into a machine sound, both sound and look in ink, on pages, we denied it was happening, we praised it.

Loving you baby was loving war in peace.

Unworldlies began to treat the blues who may never have had one blues record to love forever. The blues were like Jews. They treated a name from the outside of it. They were lost.

Names appeared they panicked to treat and there were real distresses, and only the wise knew the difference. They betrayed loneliness, afraid of it. The health of loneliness is as healthy as the pessimism of Miró which saves us. They betrayed the lonely. They were afraid of us. We were like the poor. They were afraid we might be them few years, soon else report on them, tell on them where they came from.

Being alone, at home, was feared by the nouveau unlonely.

What if hotel rooms, as a habit, was an unknown habit with them? What if the normal cosmo daily was, to them, unknown. What if going away, to *be* lonely because Loneliness called me up one night and, Baby, Loneliness said to me on the rotary:

'Baby do not forget me, don't be a stranger,' and I came away to not be a stranger to Loneliness, and be lonely and what if that was weird to some people, like a form of art they were afraid of.

A form of heart sculpture. A form of heart landscaping. A form of heart sax. A form of heart drums. A form of heart food. What if it were *essential* to the soul. Not supervised, and safe, but get on a plane to go land and jump. I have walked out. I have waded.

I have waded out into the water, with a noose around my neck to go jump. They are taking courses, in me. They want me to assimilate to the course they took. It don't work that way. You come out into world, whenever you come into world, unprepared.

What if you looked for some luck to sugar you up? What if your luck was out on the street, looking for you? What if you were busy working on yourself, making you into a better brand of likely. And luck went home, couldn't find you? And heart asked for you in the night, and you were your own heart's Judas.

Into heaven, solved.

Lord, the state.

It's dark, Lord, and I want it to be darker. A despair I can respect. A despair you could take home to Mother. Momma, meet my Dark Night. Check out them Indigo Suedes. D'y'think'd go well with my blue cerise santeen.

I can feel Robert Motherwell, in my soul.

I can feel the light of St Jean-de-Luz. I can feel the sacred Datura Tree of the shape of the titanium Datura faceless icon amulet.

Totem of the life in a hand hanging of the sheets of wind of combed metal hair of slick light of all reflections of the inner light of the Titanium Night of the Soul. I can feel the juncture of Motherwell and Gehry.

I am going home, Lord. I am going home. Outside of paint masterpieces Motherwell is among the great philosophers.

And is not Frank Gehry as great a musician of air as Ansel Adams is? And Motherwell. He is. He is in the feeling of things. Things felt. The felt thing.

I am in that Spanish desert. I am in Venice.

I am in the dry salt Death Valley. I am in the flash flood.

I am in the white shining salt like blinding. I am Doña Quijote.

I am rising across the Andalusian sand. I am making of my heart a desert.

I am making the white shine a house. I am making a white house. An ochre one. A one with blind black windows, à la Cézanne. I am making *The Good, the Bad, and the Ugly*, in the sole desert of Spain.

I am making desert spaghetti, of myself. Pasta rags of blue mist that purple that mauve that lilac that gente blue. Into the terra cotta bounces. I am making French Quarter New Orleans cottages. I am making art. This is the life, no other. I am making blinding white.

I am sitting in the dark. I am hoping for the dusk. Baby dig that lightning. God. God is.

God is sending me Morse code. I am stuck in the horse latitudes, waiting for the downpour. I am stuck in the water thrown overboard by forces waiting for rain to come pick me up. I have laid around beside the sea in lyric suites of balcony and said Honey lick my balcony and I will come bed you with my balcony and honey want to balcony and be beside the sea.

And let me lick your abstract expressionist is that ink I see flowing from your penis, honey do not leave me and mouth out, Honey let some of that nice black ink pour on me. I will be dust. I have let the wind comb my hair. The wind is my lover.

Calm to none, at the moment. I've been banged by the sea. And bandaged. And bandinaged. And in aged brine I have been the sea's geekerama, baby, I have been a side show of the ocean floor, a blur street, call me Saint Blur, come be swim with me, 'Elegy to the Spanish Republic', your number, 'To the Sea', choice yours, Ima – you know, that's right.

This is my cave band. My wave band. My band of the sea.

This is Radio Sea. Dig Waves. Dogleg Turnoff.

Radio Dog. Broadcasting from the doghouse.

I am sending out light writing. I am writing you with sound. This is ink as music. Dogology bound.

One true nail. To be bopped by a mallet beat. To have rain put like pretty little syllabic stresses.

Baby, I will hang myself before this is over. I will be dead before the end of this lead.

It's all so pink now. The page's so pink now. If I am a cut of God on the last rewrite pretty red?

On pink I do not mind one hit.

Call me from MARS. Lady come from the Planet of MARS LUMOGRAPH 100 2B. Black and blue.

I have loved you, in blue moments. I have made you up. I have made up a little you out of paint. I have truly loved you. I had a crush. I never told you. I looked at photographs. I covered your mouth. I saw your eyes. I covered your eyes. I saw your mouth. I have loved you for how you inspired me. Divine, on earth. Let us pray. Love me, and do as you please with the Saints.

Oh baby. Help me. Oh baby help me, help me, pray with me, baby. Thing ought has changed.

Since Chicago one little January '63 and every January every '63, here's some Sonny Boy Williamson, 'Help Me'.

That a Lafayette Leake-ing his organ?

Oh walk with me. Walk walk talk. Berryhop the Lenin duckwalk, two steps 8 back 'Christo Redemptor' coming up. Dedicate 'Help Me' to my feet. Feet, wherever you are, God bless. 'Help Me', Vietnam who knew?

                                                    I hear them heat cicadas buzzing. Buzzing down. May I C-section you rain or do you want further inducing. Baby:

Pray with me.

Pray. Let us pray:

I pay homage to:

– *The Dharma Bums*

– *Desolation Angels*

– *Beautiful Losers*

– Doctor Love

– Angel Blues

- 'The River's Invitation'
- Doctor Joy
- Joy in Crepuscule
- Pine Blues
- Pine Joy
- Doctor Pine
- Doctor Regret
- Doctor Keen
- Professor Regret
- Miss Sorrowful
- Doctor Skin
- Doctor Pain
- (Dr. Day)
- Plague City
- Plague Control
- Doctor Duck
- Crepuscule Alley

DOWN – Crespuscule (3)
        Alley(3)
UP Crepuscule
      Alley
Doctor Defile
     (many pass
       pass away)
Doctor Avenue
  Defile Street
Sugar Outs
Fresh Sugar
  Sugar Alley (ex Percy Mayfield)
Meat Mall
Meat Street
    Avenue
Doctor Meat
Woo Avenue

Flirt Court
Triangle Street
Hanky-Panky Avenue
Doctor Love

Saucy Street
Love Streets
Joy Streets
Sassy Avenue
Sassy Alley
Sassy Street
Miss Sass
Miss Cheek
Miss Sauce
Adultery Street
Doghouse Alley
    WAY
(dream)
(cream?)
Dirty Street
Nasty Avenue
Little Miss Baby Brazer
Vanity Street
Curvey Street
Shapely Street

Glamour Alley
Rue de Glamour
on Glamour Street
Doctor Drole
Vulgar Angels
Well-Built Street
Endowed Avenue
Callipygous Street

Rapture
Ravishing
Glorious
Devastate
Ecstasy
Spell Street
Ecstasy (3) Avenue (3)
Heart Street
word: gusto
        Relish
Earthy
base
Ardor Avenue
Gusto Street
Bone(s) Bre
Breath Alley
Thrill
Flutter
Kick
Charge
Transport Street
Abandon (3) Alley (2)
Steaming Steam
Wake Street
Fever Street
Wild Alley
words re feelings – and cooking!

Stir, need, soften, move (penetrate), divorce, (relish), desire, savour, taste, Cordial Street, *Place*, Dog Place, Dog Street, Exchange Place, Breath Alley, a-gog, a-tingle, all a-stir, all a steam atwitter atizzial, You embolden me, baby, Childe Regret, Momma Regret, Little Miss Baby Brain, Bone Way, Glamour Hounds, Glamourous, Glamourama Hounds, Angels Scum, Angel Dregs, Scum Angels, Salty Spivey, Sassy, Hussy, Jade,

House, Chippy Tart, Doxy, A Lickerish Fog, Angelhouse, Sun dregs, Robber, gangster, thug, thief, jailbird, hound, creep, mother, Lust Slut, Lust Scum, Angel Lust, Lust Dregs (no – too poetic) Lust Hounds, Angel Hounds, Angel Mothers, Lust Beggars, Angel Humidity, Fever River, Abandon River, Felicity, The Beggared Heart, Heart beggars, The Goody Gangster, Streets of Joy, Den in Sink,

Doghouse Alley
Doghouse Way
Dog Place
Dog Street

Earthy Street, Ecstasy Avenue, Rapture Alley, Heavenly Stiffs, Recording Angel, Gusto in Crepuscule, Sugar's Daddy, A Jade Yarn, A Tale For Daddy, Jade House, Angel Sink, Scumsink, The Gangster Goody, The Gooddy Stiff, The Goody Gangster, The Gangster Goody, Faffy Way, Corpse Angel, Sugar Doll (T. Williams *Baby Doll*), Graveyard Jade, Graveyard Sugar, Daddy Way, Daddy's Spoon, Daddy's Sugar, Canyon and Fungus, Celestial Stiffs, Tall Single Sugar Daddy, Big Bertha Cool, Fair Way, ScuzCats, Bone Cats and killer Kitties, Bone Cat Blues, Plague Eyes, Pretty Plague Eyes, Miss Mould, Cat Blast, Bone Blast, Night Blast, Dog Night, Nurse Scuz, Dirt Rising, The Guardians of Crime, Doctor Dirt, Rot, Lady Rot, dirt, filth, scurl? soil, grime, muck, smut, mud, scuz, rot, slop, trayf, Smut Cats, Dirt, Meat, Dirty Eyes, Dirty Baby Blues, Them Dirty Baby Blues, I'm a like, Cordial River, Doctor Diddle, Vanity Cat (s) Keen Kitties Plague Cats, Dr. Cat, Doctor Cat, Doctor Night,

Sweet Dirty Eyes, Sugar? Lady Necrosis, Love Street, Felon River, Plague Venus, Daddy's Callypigal Condition, The Galingal Gal, Mercy's Yarn, Daddy's Callypical Commotion, Momma Plague, Momma River, Plague Momma, Momma Court, Dugs, Hanging Dugs, Dog Day Fugs, Lover Rising, Lady Callipygous, Callipygous Kitties, Bubo Day, Bubo Baby, Mars Lumograph,

Slum Plague

Bad Honey Eyes, Street-Corner Hands, Plague Ecstasy, Incarnate Invitations, Koyach Corners, Koyach Clobber, Badwater, Baby Blue Dirt, No Lover No Matter, Lover Blast, Blast Abuse, desert, poverty, rot, Night, momma, bones, blast, feeling etc., Slumograph,

Poor Versus Broke

Dear Professor Regret, Baby-Blue Dirt Haze, Ahead Of us With Joy, (my) Blast Abuse, Anchoritic Angels, Sugar Outs, Sugar Oust, Sugar Aboves, Gusto Days, Pain al gusto, Rat, pain night the beaut, One X Two-Way Gusto, Street-Corner Hounds, Coffee, Coffee Goat, Pain Nightgown, Fever Meat Streetcorner Concrete, Sugar On The Streetcar, The Ex Car, Bone Night, Rats At Sunset, Beautifu , Reptile Lover, Reptile Love Saloon, The Anaphylatic Angel, Van The Man, Presz, Pres, Les Pres, Near Pres, Pres Night, Pres Or Prez, The Defile Pass (Way), In a baby-blue dirt daze, Out and About With Sugar,

Out And About The Sugarhouse

Pain Night in the Desert, Reptile Love Balloon, Old Gusto Days, The Gusto Road, Fungus and Gusto, Beloved Scuz Cats, Gimee Fever Meat, Ecstasy in Crepuscule, Two-Way Gusto, Fust Way, Fist Way, List Way, Lust Way, Lost Way,

Rapture Alley

The Beggared Heart

Doctor Dusk

Dig Them Dog-Day Dugs

Sweet Clementine Callipygous

Fever Meat

Blur Street

No Lover, No Matter

Bone Night

Slumograph

Professor Regret

You embolden me, baby. You embolden me big.

The sadness was prolific in spending my love.

My stomach was in knots from morning to night.

The blue ate the sky, and the sky ate my throat. And the colours of the cottages rose, and it all pressed down purple and tall clouds wrote. I been loving you a long time. I been waiting for your call. Give me a call. Call me up. I been missing you. How ya been. Oh nuttin', by me. Nuttin' going on. The regular. Usual. Same. No. Nothing new. Same old-same-old suicide. Life is and would a mountain go into a matchbox. CCome down real small, and come in Momma's Little Matchbox, with me. And suicide makes three. And murder is two little syllables. And kill is sweet one. And sex, one too. And violence, depending on pronunciation and will-of-the-day two, or three. Lord, this is Mrs Lonely's on Love Street coming atchoo. Thank you. No problem. Give me a call. I'm fine. Saint Augustine is *(Suicide 3 Syllables No Wait)* waiting for your prayer and I hate the bright but I love the hot. And I hate the sun but I love the heat. And I hate the blue but I love the grey and I hate the summer but I love the thunder. I am waiting for Ts to rain down on me. But first I love the wait. I love the electric air before disasters. Did I die in Andrew? Did Andrew hit? What's going on? Where did I put August? I swear I had August here a minute ago? Did I put it? Did I leave it did August slip down under the bed? Is August in the bed. I think I have to think about this a bit, and sleep. I think I'll sleep on where August went. Close your eyes. Let me slip. Find me wherever August went in the morning – in the af – I do not know why we are, but it's beautiful.

Live and direct, live and let love. I am. I peeped them in the lobby first. I have always loved to just sit and watch men come in and out of elevators. Come, in and out of elevators.

There are guys whose eyes tell you you been telling lies, to your own heart, in and out of the new found intimacy, scary, of elevators, in cities, and out. Which the vertigo of, in addition to which is much like flying with the ears blocked, and that drowning. We rode across the sea salts of shine. We rode out into the sand mirages. We rode off into the mirage sky blue. We rode off into the far mirage of the blue haze bent horizon, up the elevators of gold into the sky, provisionally high, but desert all the same, and things in the close environs of a small hotel room of gold, enclosed, occluded sight into some sort of blue daguerreo-, baby, -typing. We fumed war and still we ached. We put down the mercuric faces on the glass the desert of gilding, and still we ached for the faces which we made. I sat a long time and I walked out, off into the gallery, and I sat and looked down over the big spreading white trumpets just come from pods into trumpet shofar skirts into being, and I walked down the white stairs into the white air sun aching to rain, & I saw the white ginger white butterfly blank butterfly faces, & I saw up the lemon white faces of the Datura skirts & I walked down the pink wall to the black gate & I looked out into North Rampart & I peeped a white United, idling & I felt an action in front bit down & the Mr Big on the bench looked up seeing my breathing & he said, 'Hi,' & I said, 'Hi,' & I walked back up the pink wall through the reflecting white & I went up the stairs & sat out, & came in, & waited for this white page to go pink. I liked that Hi. It was a kind of a Franky-Hi. A Hi with one official syllable, out in the open background as an underground spoken Hi – Hiah with a whisker of a whisper of a y – a Hiah(y). That officially two letters three syllables.

3

... ... Dusk came fast but in a slow way. There was an extreme sense of well-being. Clowns rode by talking on skateboard outboard inlines talking to walkers and making for up & down speech going by & passing. There was an extreme state of well-being, like before you die. Only you didn't die. You kept on living having this extreme sense of aura before you die. You kept feeling dying but living. A great tree like a dream tree appeared like a trunk for a chair for repose. Things came in scale, & tiny. Far off dogs' blacks rested as puddles in green pastures, groomed, and cars' red lights drove themselves far off down green hills and up through darker green trees covering and the sense of well-being counterposed with the sense of immediate death − there was this harmonics of dusk, blue through blown teeth sucked up and down the streets and harps made the streets. The streets were made of the notes of the blues and the notes of the blues were the houses. On stoops steps provided for the indigent. On stoops humans came out into God's warm room. On stoops this pain inside it was a sacrilege who analysed San Juan de la Cruz and left their own love-pain out, of. Was that on stoops the pain closed in and the closeness — the pain close din and yet the closeness of every breath, of the stoop, and side by each cheek by stoop jowl humans found a kind of a kind reposing as if the great close room outside was, in summer, provided some benefit as yet to have been as of yet announced. And everyone was in the great hot waiting room of God, waiting. And a kind of ease, yet painful. As if it was – were not known yet – would the aura take over, and bring that night blindness of cars' headlights blinding you into a kind of a calm wildness, or would it all dissolve. Would ganglion love in that extranumerary mauve and strangle you at night, dead, in your cradle, or would you go out dancing, in an unknown place, with an unknown guy who had a leather holster full of God's blues teeth. Or would the still life of sitters melt in a kind of paint humidity of the Great Colourist, Himself maybe perhaps melting, by now. Or the other. And you did not know what the other was, although somehow, somewhere, someone might let you know, you supposed. If you were the supposing kind, which you might have to consider how many supposes would stand on stilts in a stiletto Tshower, coming tomorrow, They said. It was yet the hour of the universe, for a moment, when They was trusted yet, and in the calm we waited.

Some, sitting emitted in their bones blood covers of red neon nights like swim fishes' oceans all lit with the desire for love already increasing over them like their blood was skin neon shining out to those who only yet knew it like Marrano hidden neon desires for nakedness as calm as could be with a smile of flashing lewd sweetness, & the sense of a dark place with no lights all night in a dark corner of a city woods of water on a stoop & ganglions walking sulphur dogs on by all noosey.

You were an impossibility before I met you. Now you are mine, in my mind, & I hope we meet. Boy I got them terribly needy déjàs, tonight – call me. – along the feeling of how the blood neon spoke to itself. Like calm water dreams of water wave wildness in a city & it being more blacknesses in the spaces, & more sand – & such dreams as are stoops are made of. Once your first reader is no longer your lover your love has changed. Once your first reader is a listener, something else of your chest, & your breath has come into it. Desire has no excuses. Desire desires to make dreams come true. Darling, I have had dreams of you, a long time.

I'm afraid to see you, & that excites me.

I am scared to be in your aura, & that turns me on.

I'm a little terrified of what my heart will tell me.

I want you to know, I know already what my heart will tell me.

It told me just now.

Who are we who cannot be classified in the clinical words which hold love at a distance?

Who are we who cannot fit into the words of easy philosophy?

Who are we who are the children of *The Moviegoer?*

We are lost light fragments of the soul love of Walker Percy.

Which is by way of saying

You thought at first the slow summer city street

Which is by way of saying:

I – which is by way of — baby, I miss you.

4

(...... ...... Coming down into the Tommys with the cab lit aflame into my doom of the fate of it all that we can be able to choose the way we play our music but we have nothing to do with the music we get to play.

(At all into the corposant of all doggies like ships of red hot burnt on far distant blue flame horizons of the desert gone down into:

(In the dark inner repose ——

—— of the cab all jumped up with déjà vu its heart ajar feeling first time lit bits the radio's on saying,... ...

'... Just hanging here, honey. Just hanging. Honey I can never tell stories, unless I'm trying to seduce you. Just hanging on the phone. Maybe make that on a with. Just cording my gorgle, petite.

'Let me reet you a little Jackie Wilson for your — you just lay back and enjoy it. So. .... So the man calls her up. Her name? Mercy. Sister – Mercy.

'Mother, Sister,

'Momma – say 1037 on the –

'Love say dial.

'1037 on the frequently modulated Love Band.

'Just keep that uv in your arm baby

'and let the uv swing –

' – I been hoping you'd let me talk to you,
'do a bit of storying some time.

'Glad you happened to drop by now. When the dark night of your soul is back I'll be seeing you in all the familiar haunts, until then this is Mercy on the Loooooooove dial, remember nine ohs on Love Street, Love Street'll be back in the darkest time tomorrow now it's time for the Tom Udo show, here's Tommy, hey Tom U. What you say, got plenty of nada happenin'?' (Out of the swamp bright landing language of light love is, first time in, and light on the skim scum in all green by the low hot water the plane landed and the dark cab was in the light lit speckles of the last of the ear pop allowing.

Better ear purchase on radio-the-following,) ' .... '
'Thanks Dark Street for handing over that soul baton, some days you just want to put love in a chair don't you we're here with okay who's the what mosquito we got wants to slobber some saliva over the airwaves.... ... I see we got that pest on the line, oh go ahead.' 'Cecil Taylor or Cecil Fielder.' 'Oh that's cute.' 'Cecil T. Or Cecil F. Say.' 'Johnny I say Ray or Ray Charles no better Johnny Ray – Johnny Bench or Johnny Ray – NEXT!' 'Aretha Franklin or Ben –' 'Hogan'. 'I have been.' 'Oh you flirt I can see that citrus disease between your cords – get off you wide wale let someone else – any callers on the UV — .' 'What do you think of this fever – .' 'You're saying am I a denizen of the quarantine – the my or do I think coffee's to blame.' 'Something like that. You see them with all that coffee down the – .' 'Down on Thelonious Avenue. Seeing them piano rivers.

'All L'il Schools' Slight RotTaos, sure. Oh yeah goes without – next! — Talk to Tommy you want lay your lips on my gun – Go:'

'I been taking epecuhuac.' 'QUACK! NEXT! But more a dark thing I desired. Light close irony-banishment. Go!' 'I am going to put aside what I was all prep – to —

'I've been taking that epquack and I'm feeling much better.'
'Go – Nazz up your nose – go bleed on the green until the red's fluorescent, go suck your own little lunchbox leechdown – You're telling. Me vomit makes you who *are* these – Eddie Al – go – brother. Swinging Maria Rojas and the East River Murders. Go, E.A.!'

Time is ink, and 6 secs is three lines. Raining.

'I got refused in marriage last week from a woman who led to me to – the dust and the decomposition, who led me to yield to temptation. Took off that key "Not".'

'Yeah we got the picture. Down in them daguerreotyping elevatory horizontal ben'n'sweetsy bopsquawks slowed down to "It Never Entered My Mind", in the feeling. ST. LIP. Only getting-by, only surviving; and in the Mercy Kingdom of that: Only. Than a madman a girl say, to the alley gaining, when we were sand, and in the garden ends. And you were roping that day. A simple's blackened noose. No white neese, after Labour. Summers as you were back in bed-homers. Back homing.

'When you came, *Bah!* you were sent, beside yourself, in silence you tread in summary worse. Radio balm and get in the radiocab, and drive on. This is going out to Mercy out there from the graveyard, this evening, rooms have been waiting for me, baby, listen to Tommy, here. Waiting for me, waiting for you; just us. No justice, just "Just Me, Just You", waiting; rooms have waited to be enflamed by your divine lunglight. To feed the walls back to their lonely. Rooms have. Walls have made the journey to foreign lands. And studied how to spy on you. This is Tommy, sending out your noose to you, tonight. I'm sending out – Vermin and Vermiculite! Mesmerizers and PlusSized Down Egg Albumen Temporizing Paint Azimuth Sisters of Sizer-Drivers! T.O. Egg-Size The Egg-"Rock Around The Clock"ers-Egg Tempera Paint Vets of the Art Wars of 1950-T.O. TimeStop Paint Brass Rail Town Tavern Lester Young Sitings, and seeings in person, outside of the Lit-Official stories gleaned from official Art U. sources, of what foreground artists painted with, while we downtown art hounds of any old paper bag will do in a need-emergency used egg tempera '50s as always, and hung with the palette knife the sax is, when it's Lester, and the subaudition of your very artbreath, breathing:. Your walls went off to learn to look in on you. I am sending out your room to you you are in you are too shy to speak out loud to. (In the duo a word and a wall is.) Tommy the Prox. Go suck some other suicides' bones, you biographer! Go get creamy for some other corpses' details. Let us commit to the old-fashioneds. Alone and lonely, and independent. Reach out, dear Mercy, I can hear you listening there at home, right here in the radio studio. I can hear your co-breath. I can hear you listening, in that old warvet way. This is going to a particular friend of mine we used to know each other times gone by and war coverage, though I confess, as some of you may know we oh oh so only recently met. Shepp out them Itchy Archies on Mouth Blow Court, yeah what's your resto, Pedro?! What's your Barco-Balto?

'You wearing Basic Basque tonight, Eddie, baby? Eduardo. Alain. LITTLE EDDIE ET LOS ALAINS, with some "Worm or Worsty Rinse Crack", off the *You Better Kick Your Ass off the Toll It Took off of My Never Mind Heart, I Been in These Ass-Toll Weakenings, in Other Words*, I adore thee.

'Edy! Eddy! Los "Edy"s! M. et Mme Poesia. Rabbi Thelonious! Switchhit me your rabbit! Give me some of them laid down AC out of D.C. –– Keys.' – 'And then she said no to my proposal, then my girl died suddenly of the gallop, – then I believe I have contracted either the herp, an unremitting feverish burp, diabetes, a brain tumour as yet in the undiagnosed upstairs and I could be hypoglycaemic, and then I rode my gold barenaked "Berenice" sax teeth on down into the gold desert where they're going to kill me; she refused my marriage, I put myself in a shopping cart, Tommy, and asked you to take me on home, finally. I met Doctor Mingus on the sands.' 'I hear you,

Eddie Baby.' 'I said, "Doctor C., I am on the last train out of
Baltimore. I'm calling from my cell in a seat heading to Baltimore, right now."' 'Desert stuff. Good stuff. Good thing. Down
in the observant *Jerus*.' 'Riding the Human Conditions out
down below in the low below sea level muggy Mulligan
reaches.' 'Yeah. I'll say. Been worse than that in the small crap
warnings. In these Canaan Days.' 'I'll say. Tell me.' 'Dog *star*.
In the canine Canaan Days.' 'It took six seconds to kill the President.' 'You know it did. I been aching a long time.// And
before that we were treated to some of those Tom Zé brass fire
mountain far mountain brass coat clockworks out of the fine
pounded damage of démange white blanks of dalechihulyy
blown glass mob riots in the beautiful. And the small occluded
human shortcomings we are we have to pound into flaws.'
'Consigliare's a word.' 'Consigliare's a great word. Sky consigliare. Consigliare of Sky. Aestivating sky. Sky aestivations.
Sky aestivation-stations, of I been hibernating for your love in
my sneaky torpor. I been a Samurai of the Aestivating Summer
Blue Ones. Compete with my syllables, baby. I'm wagging one
now.' 'Sinatra does more in a break than some humans in
thousands of trees sacrificed to show they visited the forest.'
'Sinatra Lives IN THE breath-pauses. His breath *pauses* are sexier than some girls' entire treatise on sex. His many FFFFFFFF
never mind words.

   'Mercy! *letters*, Mercy! HIS NINE, SAY, BALLPARK, add-ons
of f's are sexier on 'terrifically', than some human's entire sour-
egg oeuvre. Active them sin syllables!' 'In the time it takes to
kill the President, 6 seconds, it is the time to say, "Here with
'The One I Love Belongs to Somebody Else', The Great Consigliare of Sky," they shot the President.' 'Eddie Al, dig it. The
sonata of Sinatra we are competing with is that, "Well now...
... – ," offhand offhandedness so nonchalanted so as to appear
an immobile fever. Before Michelangelo Antonioni, there was
Sinatra and his *L'Avventura* rocking. Entire islands swang.'

'Sinatra Strombolis.' 'Them mahvellous things.

'Terrifically, such an 'f.' We should all. Could we be. Did we do. Deed we might. Do that 'f.' Do it good. Darn it swell. Damn it down. Never dampen. Not once. Could not. Did do. Won't say. Could fritz. Could fry. In the *"Sparky"* Trap.' 'I went to the Sparky Dream Academy.' 'Eduardo, I believe you did.' 'Blue d'état.' 'Metro d'état-ers.' 'They couped the blues, they researched the Jews, they look up the guns, they wrote up little warnings.' 'They never cooed the blues, they never blued the Jews, they never heard the guns, they were dilettantes of massacres and assassinations.

'They never took their research tuchas on down to see the witness swing and travelling bring up the corpse and witness sings, Lonely Heart, I am with you.' 'Is this Radio Desert?' 'Radio Desert we be. Do not desert me, going out to Miss Mercy.

'Out there, do not desert me, baby, we been in too many Desert Wars, together: "You-and-Me". And before that we had "Blues for Yolanda", with Ben Webster and Coleman off the Hawk. And before that in our "Yolanda" suite, we had Pablo Milanés with "Yolanda", and then we way back had a little Francisco Cespedes, with "Como Si El Destino", off the *Vida Loca*, off from that Esperanto there on Lincoln Road Mall I got across from that Cuban Joint kitty-kat mall walk by the ecumenical bougainvillaea corner. By Yucca and we had some _____ .' 'I been déjà lued.' 'And I been déjà hued.' 'And I been déjà renewed.' 'And I been Lestered.' 'I been Dijon Vued.' 'And I been naked, wearing mustard.' 'I have been a pickle gherkin movie extra riding a side saddle in a western American Spanish Desolate Robert Motherwell Clint Eastwood desert Spain stretch of spaghetti sage, all rolled out, and still she would not, Tommy, love me.' 'You got your stirrups checked lately?' 'And my anvils. Everything checks out.' 'Well then.' 'What then?' 'Oh, then.' 'Not then?' 'Not much.' 'So get off the phone?' 'Could do. Might.' 'Might do. Could. Should I?' 'I would.' 'Give someone else a chance.' 'Be an idea. Be good, be swell, be nice.' 'Be right?' 'Be fine. Be Merciful. Then we had some more Beny Moré you see two-nned inaccurately, on *El Inigualable*, with "El Conde Negro", and before that the Moré of "Mulata Con Cola", then we had Caetano Veloso off that Fellini tribute CD with "Chega de Saudade", – I woke up in the iron ribs, more Ribbie slammed me, than R & B, calling, *"Bertolucci on down the raining!"* – then more off that perfect- for *Hasta Que te Conoci*, "Se Me Sigue Olvidando", then we had Silvio after Joan with off the *Sombras de la China*, "Me Gusta Todo De Ti", – except *you!* – everything-c.v., about you, except *yourself;* Silvio with *Canciones Urgentes*, the Grand Exits of Silvio Rodriguez, with a little "Playa Giron", for those thinking of taking in some *"Tango"* cola, colita tonight; feeling back to the '60s, in that São Paulo military-feeling; feeling the April October was, the November of June, B.A., between the military and the transition; when everything songs said meant everything they were meant to mean; to reveal, by hiding; to be a secret code among lover-rebels, and resistant pockets of art and vein-lovers; like sex, danger of the radiation of the people's meanings, amongst each other; for if every thing is not the flesh of a girl, and every place a deception of love, among human and maps, lovers; then we had Pablo Milanés in his, with his *Ao Vivo no Brasil* with Chico Buarque participação, and "Creeme", and we were back to the beautiful fabrication tomzéy defect with a few of his "Defect"s. And we all in our modern gnostic rot rooms of fine defect verdigris, of the untimid ceilings and the full fulsome sound resistance of the older walls, feeding the sense of that acoustic ghost of people once alive tortured and loving, in rooms back to us; ken. Kin. And out the Kinship Waves, less humanity than humannesses. And the live Beny Moré and radio in Cuba came in in between the egonschielische skyscraper black thighs, and that matissey red net *Estudio Rojo*, & then came that Radio Space known as

the Supreme Court of Art & Moré from CMQ-Radio Progreso –
Década del 50. Let me be your total compañera – you can take
me anywhere. More with "DEVUELVEME EL COCO." Radio
difusión out of Habana. *Creation*, on up into it you know what
I'm?' 'Sure. No bet. Is fine.' 'Go way. Don't leave. Come on.
Come back. Da-da.
'Go down. Get lost. Get off. Go stuff. Shoe-me. Who knew?
Shoe out, shoe in.
'Beat off, come down, get nice, go buy. You gotta you know,
so long and as long as you are: – Beat it, please stay, bye-bye, go
on: get out, come home; come on home, to me. And only me. I
confess I am guilty of the rap of love.' 'And if it love, let it be
love?' 'Exactly.' 'For irony....?' 'Irony blows and irony shows
and irony nasals and irony placells, but irony never loves; it
can't; its very breath belies it.' 'Believe it.' 'I do.'
'I know you do.' 'I know you know. Baby there is nothing for
you now but Lord Buckley. Oh – Lord! Lord! Oh Lord....'
((Coming down NINS into the garden in green dogcurbs back
wonder, like beautiful Devil Green. [Passed out of swamp down
the far dark sleep reaches of cabbing airport to city with your
eyes closed, baby, you have been there. The cab is your sweep
sweet sleep repose you do not even know you are taking it.]))
There was green of different water when you landed, doll.
There was sweet mould growing under your armpits minute
you crossed over that border dividing line of the divine customs
operation of inner plane to outer walkway and that slit. That
air slit tells you there is a heat, south, unlike any other. You
smell the tropics when you cross out over the plane. It is your
summer overcoat of aircloth, plain. It IS your tropical armour
underwear. And 'twould it be neo up on dribbling down on that
tropics, baby. Doll, it just may be. Repose, young one. Repose,
my dear. You and I, we are in this together was the air of some
presence present presenting itself to you same's me s'if air itself
got a tropical heat hard-on, wishing to rain. Down through

dark muddy sunshine and the small green sparkle reflecting bright green dots from above, once in landing were traffic signs in white and green down past the Central Business District and on ramp and on offpass and on overpass and past condo loft and undin tombstone fur chaises above on down into the hot living all still and low by high things, & close in the Quarter like houses were cottages' furniture of the room and retiring on down through in the cab where and in a feeling of brick in on down under all where it seemed brick but it was stone and wood, mostly and on under old green olive overpasses in brief large stoplight shade we have all blurred down through into the city — , I blurred down through the city hearing Tommy's show going.... .... 'I want to talk about Camille. Noose continued in the squawkbop repose. Immobile jittersies.'

'Camille's over. Forget Camille. I used to know a Camille's Fish and Chips. You want to talk flounder. Forget Camille. That dentist is over. That Magic No. 4 rivership "Prisionero d'Amor", amorcito is gonzo. Finito City. That Hurricane Dentist has passed.

'I can smell that rain wanting to come and pass.'

'I'm still thinking about her.' 'Yeah, well, I'm still thinking about me and Bob. He left me down by the flood. I been boarded, I been water-lugged, I been venisoned, I been canned Party Meat, I been patties, I been E. coli'd on down the line gut, I starved at the porcelain throne-knees, I been Lord, I did binge-ed. Hey Eddie, what's your knob?! Spill! Yeah... Bob, sure. The retirees. Don and La Doña Jubilado Huracán. Lady Hazel. Hazel No-Mazel. Pensioned-off Bad-Andy. Sure. Bob, sure okay. Bob. Bob pops up from time to time I'd rather look at my mushroom farm between this piggy had roast beef and wee wee wee all the way NEXT!

'Brassai in the morning, Berenice Abbott by night. Brassai Chez Yours-Truly, Abbott at the corner store, lonely "ALLNIGHT". Van Morrison by Dusk, Doc Pomus at Noosetime.

Cole Porter by tea, Helmut Newton at the Hotel The-The. They came after the Reds, naive and hunting.

'In my camel coat I marloneared thee, Mercy.

'I taught you, taoly, to *always* take no.

'They came after the Blues naive and hunters, yet. They liked the greens, until they found out that green in Spanish meant blue as in blue movie. And nothing having been hid from them they felt that "verde que te quiero verde", meaning what Lorca meant it to mean had been mean to them, they thought it was clean, but it was only normally lurid, of desire, in the wont. Sad, sad, sad. Sad and solitary, in this inarticulate solitariness, of my lonely, in the modern, in the heart. In wartime. Back to Peace. And the man who chooses to keep the bureaucracy going, in Peacetime, is the man who is the maquette for throwing away Freedom. And the man who chooses to be an artist because art chose him, is the Ultimate Freedom. For the man who chooses to make a thing, has his surplus value be love, and mystery and a thing, there, incarnate. But the government man, the government servant produces a surplus of keeping the state apparatus alive, and so he leaves nothing.

'Entollated mieux in the zaggerut ragrugs. HAZIN'!

'Chuzzing on down extraultra SUPER out of the rest of my oases of fressing your delicate ass.

'Come fleischdiche mornings, in the real estate sections of this life, and this flesh estate we were bourne to. *Buzz.* Optics sucked out my eyeballs and summer begged my rest. I rode the Sax of Jordan out, and I saw the word INDIGO like the flame of every stable mordant. I saw things *soaked,* SO CAKED that I began to lust, for how blues plays, and no more than in the desert New Orleans is with that restful stinging light so water-filled it misses itself in salt Devil's Golf Course mirages that it is the divine low wet place which has lost all its water and cries for it so much at night it is daily refilled with its own nostalgia like some of sweetness, so brutal. I came on up to New Orleans, when I first shot war in Guatemala you could not see. And I brought my photographs of things which were not there I had negatives of. And I brought my film, undeveloped of the things I had been a witness to which could not be witnessed in an ordiNARY MEANS.

'And those who had not been there, in time, became voyeurs of that exhibitionist kind: they wanted to hear all the details of the things they were violently not interested. They wanted it described to them, what only those who have never experienced it could describe. And so began that starvation of the heart. And so began that starving of the brain. And so began that lung starvation, and skin, leading to an odd way of talking. And so began that thing.

'Began that thing where those who wanted to know viciously and intensely. Due to precisely they had no interest, in a thing, and in the lost postango arena of us,.... Did you kill yourself? Am I the aftermatter of your solitary dream? Is this the day before, which is the night after the allergy attack, ZZZZZZOOT

'Is the world a heart attack of God, and we are the silent enzymes? – Did we die dead and be bourne coming onto this Heaven earth is, dead, at the first? If we are all dead, what is suicide? Is Suicide LIFE as Percy Mayfield said. Is living a suicidal act and killing yourself a variation? If no one on earth has ever committed suicide and come back to tell of a successful voyage, then is war the closest thing we have? Are we the war-experienced the suicides of the planet and the bumph generated by the living ABOUT we dead? Is life just a folly of the decapitated-brains talking on panels experts BECAUSE they haven't been there? Is it possible all the world and sexologists do not say whether that –

' – particular Doctor Sex is actually satisfying

' – and any good at it, sacwise....? If we all

'are all dead and this Earth a Heaven, then what would a human ideologically committed to showing their entire life you

| 113

don't have to kill yourself be?

'Might they have entered an art form *in*

'*order* to order the materials around in

'a One-Way Street? Might they be like summer? The Imperialism of the Day? Might they be like summer and optimism? And less like fall and the dark, when Night is Set Free? Might they have entered an art form, in order to show you can be a success at it, and thus failed time and over and over, at that Low Bar success is, having many rote semiriffed shortcomings, but never any great displayed flaws, for success is only an alias for conforming; but failing grandly, I confess I do not know Thy True Name.

'Or are we just into having a little "Por Amor", with Marc Anthony in the Hurricane Days –

' – are we even in the August A's of 'Canes, yet?

'Oh, lovely, be my little hottchelbrew. I dusted. My little Lucille du Maison du 'B.B.' – on: down.

'I mighta died. It's so hot I can't remember – the thing with Christopher Walken is is was he he wo whoa.

'Wouldn't but you wouldn't and we wouldn't on his to whatever not be. Oh, but dust. But then you'd. Tommy. You wouldn't want him Tommy to. To fall too deep. Then asleep on his Lip. Because you better. I'm saying watch. *After.*

'Because he falls, Tommy, too bad asleep he's going to go into some kind of slomo bebop coma, and be far.

'Too widewake then for his.

'Own you know.

'But I woul.

'Don't.

'I'm not going to.

'Be too widewake for the strange hummer, Tommy.

'That hanging tree I don't know. Whether. Brownie.

'I don't think so. Brown, *Clifford!*, T.*Tom.*

'March I'm talking 26th, '56 I tell you, Tommy. #2-6.

'Clifford Brown dies. Eldridge who else. You're talking Henry you're talking Harry, Tommy.

'Tommy, you're talking Tommy.

'You're Tommy Tommy talking Jimmy, you're.

'Tommy, talk Tommy? Sure. You're. Tommy, you're talking Dorsey talk Tommy. James, Henry you could talk Harry you're into James-talk.

'Or you're, Tommy, Tommy you're talking Jimmy you could Tommy-Jimmy; fine. You're absolutely. Know what I mean? It might Be Lester. Getting-by. Knowing the marvellous.

'Talking Frankie you're talking Dick what'shisface, you're talking Alvin, you're talking, Tommy − the President of Love, for if there were human hurt, it.

'For if there. If there were human hurt, __ might be Lester.

'If there were human hurt it might be Pres. Hurt, and forgiving in the hurt, knowing it is not *his*, to: forgive.

'If there were human getting-by, knowing the marvellous, but knowing it is not his to forgive, for travelling brings out the ghosts, and witness swings, and in war there is always love, knowing it is not ours to forgive, but in the hands of something greater.

'And war brings out the ghosts, and witness swings, if there *were* war, and it is, and we come back richened in these sick dark ways but knowing the marvellous as the true contrast now in, then, Tommy, we are in Presville now, and we can't return: having known the marvellous of being there, in our time, our place, the things and not at all ever *ours* to forgive, even this forgiveness, even forgiving at all, even the word to forgive, and that kill has one syllable and to ponder, all war's fault, for which I am grateful, otherwise I would have been going to the paper morgue to look war up, but I don't have to: I took the photograph, which made the headline, I don't have to read the paper, for if you shy back from war and world, then the paper becomes a place, instead of the pale invert sketch of breath it is, and into the Darker Alvins. Once chair, one rot, one book. One forge, one chair stamp, one table. One pencil, one stub to long for. One planet MARS LUMOGRAPH BLUE KISS TO evolve around the planet. Weenies stock up pages. Masters wear pencils down. Beginners pridefully boast of what they have accumulated. Masters say nothing, and take out their pencil, at parties, to examine how much smaller it has become so pleasing. And knowing the marvels as marvellous-us, bytimes knowing that the marvellous is only the getting-by between humans, and that we were sent here from Planet Death, only to survive, but to make that soul survival an infinite pretty. And knowing it was never the President of Love's to forgive us in advance or do anything but just Tao on Down to the Mississippi Desert. And tEDDY wILSON *swang*. And knowing the marvellous. And dogs walked. They *emulated* Don C. M. Walken. Emulating the marvellous in bars like cloud bullies. And clouds of Nola bullied on down. Dumbo Bouncers at the fold. Dumbo Bounceritos. Grossero Gordo Cloudos of Divine SkyDumbo Ursulines. The concrete street was a dead grey dog, just lying there. The cottages were the furniture. The clouds were the walls. The clouds were Reet Complete'. '(And, yes, in the canyons of New York, Udo, I heard) Jackie Wilson sing to me, for my soul was shooting now, without ever looking IN my camera, I wanted to make everything a musical object, for I had seen friends dumped on the morgue steps, and it made me want to kill Peace Ironists as of war they sang, as generalists, about groups, and making individuals not that, but just exemplars of theories. And my friends did not resemble anyone else, and they did not have such fancy fictional names. Tommy, David, Richard, Karen, Sheila, Kent, Linda, T.J. John. Chio. Herman. Pelotita. Adam. Joshua. Abraham. T. D. R. K. S. A. J. A. L. Ch. Pto. Rocio. H. Mr W. The Divine Eddie Al. JW. JC. TW. TM. LY. Lester Young who could make every word into a swing of adverb. How do you speak of things-ordinary, which involve

you die as a normal thing you assume you go to work in the morning and it's no big deal, amongst those circulating their overscandalization did not make massacres seem bigger, but far less, because of the overweenie importance in tone and choice of words those doomed to become exhibitionists, sick, extremely committed to lifelong lack of experience. You got that room of yourself, baby, but they forgot to tell you, you got to come out and live in the world, sometime.) You got to get a job assumes you die every day. And they didn't. And we did. We boomed! Baby we boomed. We made the things of the news of the day they used for their ironic distant over factstuffed storying and the more facts they stuffed in the less it resembled the real thing. For the real thing of war did not resemble a single fact you could look up or acknowledge about it, any more than a city you enter into can be known by reams of the Chamber or Metro Issues in the momentary fevers of Mother Councils. And the more fiction became fact-based the more there seemed, not less, fear of the actual world, for world when you are in it is not factual at all, it is materialist and hit the other way. Walk me down to them squawking Walkens baby, I got syllables to fry! Come here, little o, and let me introduce you to Old Sparky......
he-he .. Clyfford Still with a suitcase. Kind of John Galliano got caught in A WINDswept then halfway down that biascut Bob Fosse isolation muscular crepuscular throat stopped but I'm going to, then. And went blue paint vat, then stole up to cobalt and tried to talk it down to some night vetivert, then got hefty with the Calamus Station coos, crowd, then and all the others. Walken. Walken at the Reins. Strengthen the reins and go dead easy. Downtown BOY. (Gallo at the Station.) (OH, feed me, downtown boy with your juice!) 't and so began literature began to waste away, for it began to feed itself on facts, but, friends, literature's bread – is dreams. And so began those with the least interest began to be educated by those with equally as little interest but with more ambition and energy about the

large scale issues and tragedies, AND everyone with no interest was included, and inclusion of apathy was its name, and everyone who wanted to be more fully educated on things they had no particular passion for was a great success, and those with no passion but a great ability to will themselves forward relentlessly stockpiling facts to feed and make sick lit, taught those with as much lack of interest but less civilian-willingon, and we the soldiers of war in journalism looked at them all like they were mental cases and the streets of the cities were the claustrophobic babbling asylum, and we on the street corners saying strange things were not sane, per se, but at least we had been there; we said one name. Tommy and Mercy were lovers. Mr W, Thy Hip Divine. Eddie Al, you posed me and saved me, riding on that Blue Baltimore Train. (The Blueless Clueful Bureaucrat? He might as well as have never been. He has chosen, in democracy and freedom, to leave nothing behind you can see, *you can touch*. The Gods, today, are the men who make something, *the Gods today are the men who make something with their hands.*) And the music of the Blues Gods came on down. In this soul survival of the Getting-By we are here only to be obliged to make that *Getting-By* and make a larger sweeter Kingdom and the *Mysteries of Love*. And then the evidence began to respire on me in its low swamp autopsies and things of a shape began to intimate-me, close, in their deep involving hostage-sweat love-suffocation into that cataract feeling of the light, & no other thing & my cab eyes sweat & like wet shutters pestañas *lit* I was a cottage in a cab with wet shutter eyes & I, the cottage got out of the cab and into the room, and I was a cottage in a hallway, and the hallway was called "Love Street", and I was on the street of the room and the room was love, and I was walking through the gates of the vanguard, surrounded by things sweating in on me everywhere like a green cloth from an inner room of a long black and green and red curtain, lying down low and vertical with some yellow, and sweating out a frame of how all that palm filled my window eyes and all Moroccan in the feel of New Orleans first time, in the hot dead and forever furnace heat began & heat has never ended in this eternal August eats September & coming forward to '92 I now look back on with the magic August 24 when the 1st alphabetical fervour began the fur panics boarding & water bottle luggers – I remember Andrew when A did not hit, & I was reminded of every disaster I waited for – & the strange green light before Andrew did not hit & no body & the Quarter but the river & we light hounds in our strange low Ozone Sexing. It can take 15 years to write a book as a tourist to religions, but the Metropolitan who cares less as a Jew about sourcing himself can just start, at the 14 1/2 year mark, & take 6 months, & save 174 months, for loving. Like pylon hiders in python composing.

'And like war, when you could die but didn't but walked but others didn't, I did not know how to describe in such articulacies, how it was to live through the things, & not show damage but have damage; in démange white blanks & blankets of white blood nights with no irises only whites, & be in this thing of looking like anybody, but carrying around elsalvadoran war shrapnel & have the hot low late sun respiring be using the bullet bits by my lung for that bullet emergency purpose – of lead to write with, & inscribing me, & also the pictures – & the things which *don't* happen which are due to, too shock you; here's a little off the *Inarticulate Speech of the Heart*, "Inarticulate Speech of the Heart", with Van Morrison off the double album – And I came up to New Orleans for the first time & many repeatoffender times from the southern Americas to meet my doom, in Peace further. To find an atmosphere in Peace where Peace was being practised, as if it were wartime, & in the gratitude, of the posmerciful blessings.

'My soul needed to R & R in a Secret Death Locale of Sweet Pleasure, for the sake of my possoul survival.

'And when everybody runs and gets out of it it is we war

photogs who roam the streets of the anticipation of the sexual aura of as if it is all an inner hot room waiting for the doom of love to arrive up onto your ass as if you lay long enough with a Matisse view it began to open up into a Dufy water swing, and all stuff. And that North African feel of the air of things in the looking out and the seclusion of the –

'(I remember the flood of April '83 in the spring when everything was new and about to be over and the St Charles streetcar did not temporarily run, as water covered the tracks), as it will in time cover us all all of us at Stop 21, and I was in love with a boy a cophotographer, and (I remember when I first came north that first time it was from the wars of the southern Americas I first came north to New Orleans and cabbed in and I remember the crispness of fall in '91 November & still the Moroccan palms on Dauphine on white walls) (pinking slightly with chains) stirred me for no uncertain reason at Napoleon's, at the Napoleon House platterlouched out, days, I remember cabbing up in my arrivage smithereenitas my heart like smithers and some kind of clean door refreshment of a green door with a black door inset in it in a pale blueness revealed itself as white at first but then the blue after a while began to body forth and not so much shine as yes just reveal itself and into that blue space of the black door inset in the green door came a black door inset with a pink door and on that pink door was inset, further, a white door, and on that white door was inset a red heart and that red heart was mine and I walked into the open door of love which was the hand of love and it was mine and clean as a Matisse cut-out, in the late days of love of the material oasis of love of the material things of art of love, in the making and I remember and it came to me before I saw it rusts of other tenders these rusts and oranges all wrecked and lined striated and distressed and green triangles and kind of simple clown feelings, just tender sketches: I remember the dry feeling of summer and things drying, but even in the driest time things unable to dry.

'Having been in the wetness of their own embodiments of below sea level in some dried sea but still remembering it, as if in New Orleans in summer we are all reminiscing fishes. And oh yes walking down the green sweat gate of love I was revealed onto the walls. I was in my love for the first time and I had never dreamed of it. I was in the great unlikeliness of you. I was in this thing for the first time, forever, I had never dreamed of. For I had never dreamed of you, Tommy. And flotations like morphs of crepuscule an abode. And just wonked out moons. Haunts as fogs walked by. Portmanteau trailers hauling. Nobody and nobody. And it's always being here. Repeat still rooms and I did not know they awaited me. I did not know a thing. I did not know I loved thee. Quiet lookings for the shape of leaves. I was just arriving: past pampas grass and green pools in the brown. Even drying dead leaves seemed aching for rain and wet and overwet and begging for rain and rained on and sweated and soaking and begging to be wet still. And on and on. Even not out of the cab I knew all this in the grand unknowing. I was sweating out the replacement of the music inside me I remember there were so many summers of pouring down and wettening up a little less, and summers of begging for rain. I have been begging for rain this summer. What changes? Nothing. Wet and dry. Red paulkleeiana shone and lumiscent fish in the blue we came down in dark cabs in blue shimmers of night occlusions by day, in the feeling.

'Paul Klee shone and lumi*nescent* fish in the blue mines we came, down in cabs blue shimmerings in nigh occludes so by day in the feeling we were want to explode to stars cops rode by on horseback & could peer in upper's rooms. Palms in ink dipped their shape on white walls later revealed to be that paling blue, again. Old stained purple lettering just stained on down and leaked and revealed to the world was the word of the ancient days, early yet. In the going. Repeat feelings of *The*

Red Studio of Matisse came back to me from my many sojourns with it up in New York City over the many years, in MoMA in the just as you came in & entered the Matisse room & then could sit on the cushioned bench overlooking upside-down 53rd feeling being finding hum in Rothkoans to Mark Rothko around used to come, during work breaks to look at it, *The Red Studio* & art is the feeling of adoration which surrounds it and the clinic-feeling of it like *Last Tango* and the feeling of its having everything in it about the life of the artist, and everything. And down into Août of August & snow ripped apart in rivers of hivers of snow on the a.c. And so much just to hold, to look at, to examine, like a room of love, unbended to us and generous in its feel and still the feelings to come revealed themselves to me, as dreams the sleeper has when wideawake being accustomed to dreaming and air disciplining it down to you in these barometrical arrivals to ozone, in summer feelings of somebody save me, something save my life; arriving up from much further south & colder, the leather Junes of Florida in Buenos Aires & the high crocodile close boots & the mocshade soft suede suits & the olive high turtles of July coming north to New Orleans where a sleeve was entire philosophical conundrum: God was real in New Orleans, in August, but nobody knew if sleeves existed.

'And from the world where ordinarys of *Red Fish* went – I came – the north said work to a demeure – the north sent work – the north seemed working to a derrière-garde position – at feints of timids to mildly amusedly observe & lightly scold, in books, their protagonists as if it could be true that the future had arrived in 2001 that as in 1982 we could make the thing which in 1820 made Poe explode & Whitman burst & be the repeat as-good-as in flowery undisciplined English that Borges beat making Spanish sit up & bark à la a Raymond Chandler. /// Radio. Radio Road. B'cast St. Domestic Downtownness. Ordinary *Cool*. And while the north worked to advance, incrementally, to be in the days before Charles Brockden Brown & just after – to reach, in other words, – a quite well done flowery gothic – *which* when done sat on the shelf & in the bookstore's equality & was just as good a well done product in 2002 as in 1971 as in 1793 as in 1853 as in 1985 as any well done thing, unaware Poe had spawned Julio Cortázar or how great a downtown influence Lou Reed was on Walt. Or the Nine Inch Nails of Dread of a *Dead Ringers* I been reseeing nightly a long time, and especially with Tommy gone), nostalgic for my home town, T.O., & the very neighbourhood of my great-great-grandmother's house on Grace across from San Francisco de Assisi, off Mansfield & that old green diamonds white paint blue lit every brown brick of T.O. Cronenberg is a master of catching in the rust & brick metal zinc oxide oxblood; & load on down with me, baby, let us return life to the Creatively Lazy! Come down. Come back. Return to the hand's disease. Return to the Lord's desire. Come back to the Lord's disease. Come back to heavenly lack of ambition.'

'Me –'79 I was reviewing my Lasts then – and the first Sonny Boy shall be served as ' "Rice" Miller' what's on your mind Wally?'

'You recognized me –'

'Fellow hack –'

'It was raining that March and by June Jeff had a fever –'

'Sure. Jeff. Okay, Jeff what – Wally's bro here named after our _____ th President, Jeff Davis – the point – you up back to Washington soon we're going to have you on as a special guest on you still hanging with the reeds and the rushes and all those nice swords you're collecting with that hard stuck sticky-outy in the swords or what talk to me Wally –'

'I remember when Eddie Al and I met one time in New York City – we were sharing the journalistic trade at the time. I was checking out the ailing and the dispossessed in the wards of the necrotic sadness in D.C., in that war time ever with us. I remember the troubles in Habana.'

'Good honest work y'ever wonder today you're picking up a storying book it's like I'm, "I'm, 'What,' – 'hello?!' *he* – llo'! – '(y)'ello!'"' – been out much, lately – been out of the house – been out of your *brain* – been out in the never mind – NEXT what you got to say – rain you know what I'm saying here – go work the police blotter you're looking for to paragraph where's your at been today – ?'

'Velma.'

'Hey, Velma. I used to know a Velma in Manahatta – Velma wore hats from Jonah's nose. Go, Velma, Vel, Vel –'

'I used to date you.'

'Oh, Velma, why didn't you say I don't think so, I'm not of the Velma persuasion that must have been some other awful fershlungena farfel bow tie 5-colour set – tsk tsk y'ever think how them red bells, spinach, what is that – saffron, squid now there's some species got ink, I mean when squid and saffron rub bow ties in the night, look out, children! You the one with the cat Kimel.'

'No, that's my rye bread.'

'Well, don't go slicing that cat at the deli too thin.

'Gotta go – see my hotline's lit – Red Rot Network T.J. Udo – need healing – Keep those open wounds, yes, baby?'

'Remember me from Calamus Street. We fought sleep, together. The Sleep Wars. We were in the Brigades against The WideAwake. You and me, recall? were in the Coma Brigadistas. The Barcelona strut amps, with them ambs so sweet.'

'Oh yeah. Good stuff. Been there in Prosthetic Town. Rambling my stub, on down. We've been there. Maybe. Sure. I don't know. Sure. Maybe. Convince me.'

'You see – *Ran*?'

'Oh yeah, years ago You're talking I'm thinking wasn't that that I don't even know if I'm talking out of "Good Morning Little School Girl", or "L'il", depending on your school I'm saying here, trying to remember, okay, preference, *Ballads and Blues* I'm looking at it right now Mother – Sister Mercy left over from her Dark Night show – "Blues For Herluf".'

'Her what?'

'Her luf is as good as her warp. Maybe that's her twaffe Please Mister Webster. Speaking of which spotted any most wanted rain on the street, I'd recognize it anywhere, *Ran?* – Sure. Back when my Azulejos were in the pennant race but as usual.'

'Hey, Tommy!'

'Hey, Dust! Daddy *DUST!* Who's been dusting your bronchitis! Who *has* been dust busting your ass, a rare occasion folks – one of the genuines. One of the gangrenes. You used to dust my ass, remember back at the Hotel Intercontinental that time, or do I mean the other, you know when that what the hell *was* that guy anyways, with some agency-aid thing, and they came remind me of the hotel, we went out that day to the countryside, and they come in, they shoot the guy face-blank in the hotel coffee shop shoot him came in and shot him, because he had a beard and was yay-high and they meant to come in and shoot the priest, sitting at the other table, who didn't look like himself that day. Remember Ease Island? Remember when the sadness was too much to bear so we'd go in your darkroom and look at the red bath by coke? Remember when we used to go into the darker Saint Bookers, of the "On the Sunny Side of the Street", just to feel sick with the perversity of it all, of They and the Optimists. Remember how I used to call you up, to smoke cigarettes. Honey, you were the best listener I ever heard. You taught me a good listener knows full well to listen is a good active verb. You taught me everything. You taught me everything, about love. About "to listen". About the Two-Way Street. And war much more resembles two incredibly well-trained listeners, just sitting together smoking war down in a room. And they wanted to *talk* to us. About what? We were monkeys in a

Peace Zoo, for them. We were the active tense of their relaxation in feeling comfortable in their passive apathy fevered to a mania to hear all about what we couldn't talk about we'd gone through, in their minds, to have confirmed. Everything in war is in bad taste. They wanted it in good taste: uniformly horrible. For nothing is half so proud and proud of itself than – *as* a well-educated middle meeting another schooled middle and telling that one what they the one have been through, confirm. But it never was that way and we were the children of Mid-Century. Remember how you used to stick your finger in where your finger could fit, built just for you and that nice secure tightfitting finger, and twirl, just ABC and to the left of it, in that I. And twirl me your black vintage Bakelite Stalker, by nights, dial me up on that nice rotary cum phone, with the good sound quality, the Bakelites especially, and when in doubt are very heavy as a murder weapon, and call me and talk secure and acoustically sound. It seemed today that those on the cells didn't have much need for solace in the listening, they were always breaking up, and anybody could come in and ruin the silent heart attack you were having just catching that last wave, of the breathing remember when they blew up Somoza's Pollo Joint that time?'

'When we saw *Fingers*?'

''83 am I right?'

'We come out – *El Precio Del* or was *D'un Hombre* and there's like how many guardia whatchamas and we see that guy get just shot like walking what?'

'A half a block.'

'Max. Max half block. Max. Total maximum. Less. Truly. Maybe quarter. Maybe less. Probably less. No way half and he's like bye-bye.'

'And we're like what?'

'Six or seven steps behind. 3 1/2 seconds. Total max. Doubt even the half. Probably less than the half, but more than an eighth. 3 seconds total max end of story.'

'Wasn't a *bad* pollo joint, Somoza's.'

'You never ate there, honestly you did?'

'No but almost honestly. Once. We were almost going but we never got there, but I tasted it. It tasted like chicken.'

'You mean oh that was that time with that hit guy what was his name where we he we go he takes us we went, go that time up to his what was his name, Mr "I'm Writing the Big Novel".'

'Yeah but that's what every guy isn't wasn't in "electronics" back '70s late talking, talking late '70s early '80s all those places, countries, every whipsmart whiplash hired gun killersmart hired handgun man and U.-dangers sniper is either "Hi, my name is, I'm in electronics," or they're, "I got to go home and kill that main character," and they *killed* him, remember Franz.'

'Heinz. The guy's name was Heinz.'

'No, Heinz was Mr I Just Got a Bullet in My Arm from Hanging My Arm out the Door Driving through El Salvador, and No I Am Not a Journalist, I'm Just HERE, There's This Great Salad Place and Pasta with a Tiffany Lampshade Says JAZZ Not Too Far from Mario's Rooms You Might Want to Meet Me so obvious it hurt was guess-what, Guatemala, guess, 1980....'

'I thought that was What'shisface.'

'No, What'shisface was an entirely other face at all. What'shisface was "Sky" of the B system.'

'B-section.'

'I think it was the B-line. The this is like Central America, 1980, "... just pick up the phone and tell her who you want back in the States." "Her." "Her", mind you. Not the operator. "Her". "Her", from his apartment. New technology is rarely new. It just emigrates from geeks and government goons to civilianhood. Did he kill that girl, do you think?'

'I don't know I always wondered. It might have been our imaginations.'

'It could have been our imaginations, *and* he killed her or was it just the nextdoor sounds.'

'I don't know. We got out.'

'If we hadn't we'd be dead now.'

'We don't, we were.'

'We didn't, we're gonzo.'

'Bye-Bye City.'

'MorgueTown.'

'Necrosis with the Mostest.'

'Woundsville.'

'Zounds bars.'

'Remember that collection of platters Heinz had.'

'He wasn't Heinz. Heinz wasn't Heinz. Heinz was the other guy. Mr Jazz Tiffany Lampshade Gangrene Bullet Wound Doper of the High Valor. He was an idiot. But he wasn't Heinz. I mean he was. But who you are referring to as Heinz was What'shisface.'

'Oh yeah. You know I always forgot. I forget that Heinz isn't Heinz. Yeah, he had an immense record collection. He had that vintage mint Charlie Chan Debut which you tell me.'

'I know. He was Swiss, not German. Mr Record.'

'I wish we had some record rains. I been feeling like it would be nice and fine if it could be, today, like San Francisco that other February with that record rainfall, and L.A. was crying like that what'shisface in *Chinatown*, the guy who drowned in the L.A. desert, looking at the sea. You know. But it's true. No but it is. Yes not but it's true; no but it is. I never saw anybody with as many records.'

'Not a speck of dust.'

'That guy dusted his dust without any dust tell me that.'

'He had dust *to* dust and he did comply.'

'He dusted his dust 'til his dust cried for must and still you never saw a speck of dust, on them remember "All of Me", when he played it that time I walk in that green ether atmosphere you're sitting there with that Hungarian.'

'He was all Czech.'

'Yeah, yeah, they're all all Czech he was Hungarian. The "novelist". Him and about ten thousand other hitmen. Him and about every snoop. Every snoop and every spook every lame brain unlamé, even a TV spy was a novelist then. Remarkable that the keynote of a dirty silent brutal war, where the known covers are "electronics", and "He's writing a novel", in every bar they're waiting the order to kill someone, is now in the north.'

'And they don't even know it.'

'I like that.'

'You're sick.'

'I am. But I still like it.'

'You always liked sick things.'

'I do. Did. They keep me healthy. People who stay away from sick things always seem anorectic. They're starving on good taste.'

'Yeah yeah yea yeah yea. I loved that "All Of Me". It was nifty. Whose "All of Me" was it.'

'I think it was Ben Webster.'

'Off the *Soulville?*'

'Could have been. Right time frame. But they do. They don't know that someone who is "writing a novel", when everyone is "writing a novel", is known to those of us who have lived through regimes as note-for-note word-perfect note-on ear-on dead-perfect mimicking a low-rent Hit Man with the known code transmitting what he does. So it works for us, and they get to work for the government, for free, and not even be paid for the known worldwide words that say they are evil 'cause guess what they never came out with it.'

'Or naive.'

'Same thing. Works for the government. Works for me.'

'I don't think it was Ben Webster. I think it was somebody

else. I don't know who but it was.'

'But who?'

'I think it was Lester Young. Gotta be Pres. Feels like Pres inside me. Feeling very Presidential, of late. Very Algiers. Very Miss Algiers. Very Miss Belzonia. Dust my Broom*s*! If there were human hurt it.'

'Gotta go.'

'Catch you on it – might be the downdraft. Pres if.'

'Lo-fi by, baby. There were. Lo-fi that desert. – Might be Lester.'

'For but. Be lonely but remember – be: surviving is this thing need human, do not scold us for getting-by *Is* be good.'

'Betcha. Desire me, somatic in your lullaby. Love you. Need ya. Bye-bye.'

'Bye. For living brings out the artghost & thinking brings you zero. And facts of an era give you nothing; just a better fear of failing, so you don't. But live in a prison of research, making of facts a totalitarian body. Somatically breathing the ledger keeper of mistakes made you never made we the Reader have been longing so to see. Even fame, or riches do not bring an artist to Great Thrilling Chances. They never took them poor & unknown, they never take them, after. Only War teaches you Love. Only dark abate evidences dark on note evides dark intimate evils teaches you the good is unreachable. And witness *doth swingeth*, & maybe is for a nonchalantingness but if you, and maybe is for nobody else but you, Childe Art.

'One of the originals, folks. One of the best. We had our times. We were *there*. If you were there, you're an exotic, in your own country. And your own country is prepared to love you, as long as you keep your mouth shut. And your country is prepared to be loyal to you, as long as what you say does not get your country in trouble. And your own country loves you and pledges its loyalty to its love of you, as long as you do not say that Paisistas tend to give war vets the creeps. And only the lonely war vet knows precise as a war surgeon the difference between loving your country, and that kind of conventional-wisdom of unfun nationalism's conventions which snides and sneers and sarcasticizes and ironizes and self-praises and self over highly apprises and and is the same old timid bully boss-ing around the small landlocked duchy of the mind in an art-lock, pleading its bullinesses as inferiority when it always much more dangerous: Beware the Raging Timid. And I began to speak, out of my throat last and first things, in Spanish pic-tures, which came out of my gorgle, in Saxon. Not a translation, Lover, but emotional English for Spanish tonation, of heart. My second language became my first, inside, but I looked like you, and you did not understand me in my native throat, for my heart hit the syllables some other thunder. And I been feel-ing, friends, sad of late. So many small pieces I had to box in baby's coffins, of grown men I had personally loved, and had inside me, and done drugs with. I had toked on a Tuesday, and on Wednesday I found them tortured and cut up. And this is what the regular everyday middle-class person you went to school with, who is just like you, no higher nor no lower, chose to do, and would not have done any other: we brought you the stories of the fronts and the battles, and then you called us the media. You used us for your research and the research over-showed, but you used us, you abused us, you used us, you needed us, you propped yourselves up, with us, you used us, you overused us, and when you were finished with us, to hide your evil naive heart, you pretended you had never had any-thing-at-all, to do with us. Novelwriters, you used us, and then you were the most rabid saying everything and all you chose to do was our fault. You used us and then you called us The Media. But the finger was pointing right back at you. We were the same as you, and we went, and you didn't, and you didn't know, but we did. Here's a little something for others of us who went, when you see out on the street we look just like you, and

there is no way of telling, here's some "The Thrill Is Gone".
With B.B. King. Oh baby that thrill keeps going so fine, each
time I love to go back and have it be gone gone gone, again.
Linked by direct kinship to "Besame Mucho". Baby let that
Ultima Vez vez me on down to that last ultimate time out of
mind and again and again, I'm telling you honey, I survived
war on a hell of a lot of "si fuera"s. Tell ya.'

'Let me be intimate with you.'

'The very heart of the cur of it.'

'I used to see you what was it over on OY and UR or. By the
Royal phone. And the lost feet tiles. I been feeling kind of you
know, liturgically shmata, on the Samurai side. Very
Rauschenbergian, of no one ilk, and sea-open.'

'OY and AN....'

'Oh yeah, that's right OY and AN at the A & P I used to run
into you picking up something hot down that Rue ___ aisle
wasn't it?'

'Okay, we lost the corner of OY and AN momentarily, maybe
he got hung up down in the feminine hygiene group. Talk to
me.'

'Tommy?'

'Yes?'

'Remember me?'

'Remind me.'

'I was feeling bad.'

'Okay Feeling Bad, how's Feeling Bad feeling this afternoon?'

'Much better.'

'Good. Fill me in.'

'I killed myself last night.'

'I'm not surprised so how're feeling now.'

''bout the same.'

'And?'

' "And?" '

'The point.'

'The point? What do I do now?'

'Where's your pain at?'

'I'm hanging on the phone.'

'By you mean you're saying.'

'I guess that's right.'

'Locate yourself. Corner of X and What?'

'Corner of Low and Medium.'

'Twirling you're saying.'

'Not a lot.'

'But a little. Low speed.

'We got a low speed gorgle twisting – honey, how far are you from the bed, can you see the bed.'

'I can see the bed.'

'Well, darling you made your noose go hang in it. NEXT!

'You. People. You know, people, my policy. Self-sufficiency, independence, honour the word. You going to kill somebody, do it. Kill that man. You going to kill a somebody's you, go right on ahead, have nachos. Kill yourself. You going to kill someone, stay out of it, get brownie points, no sentence, no accomplice, no nada, he dies, you live, you walk, I'm sorry, you one of them Goody-Two-Shoes keep your funk for some fun on the – ones, hokay? You going to kill yourself, kill yourself, live with it.

'I see my faithful producer's waving her juicy half-Muff at me, gotta go, man I can feel that Extra Virgin already I'm thinking here's Bobby coming in right now earn his bread, Bobby, Bobby, I see you got your buckets in hand, folks like a clock, one white, one black, bucket in each hand here comes Ma Bobby, Bobby don't Rob me, just mother me well, in the night, I'll be back when the sun shines darkest don't worry I'm just going to wheel myself right out that window, again, this is your own private Udo saying, Keep giggling, and keep those nooses on high....'

'DeepDish Doctor Duration, The Lady Doctor is Sin! And

dogs lay down for breakfast, and fish swam; world has been tender in its rebuttals. And world has been tender in its retribution. Tender Retribution. Tender Punishment. Oh, world is tender in its rehabilitations. And just rhythmic interiors over the sea. These tender things which rip me up now into tender rags, this very night. And the sky just keeps tearing itself apart in tender shivas. Tender Rents. Uptown Trash. Billionaire Garbage. Mansion Squats. Mansion Midtones. Take me, Lord, to my Umbraclum, I beg You.

'I am looking for an old green colonial tint. A soft lime celadon at last. A kind of an old wine, in velour but much more matte. The veils of straw. The mould of aerial views dilute. I want rot worm mould, but softened. I want a green necrosis in my curtains. I want gangrene but in velvet. I want bruised zinc. I want to amputate parts of me, because they keep getting in the way; like my brain. I want my voice to come to you, direct from the open neck. Last song 'til morning. Just that old colonial gold. Just that gold, in after-noon. The Ultimate Bath. Sailing on past peeks out shutters, in that jalousie thrill of light so subtle in the shutter stick adjustments, it could be reality in a thrill, of nothing.

'And things roughed, peeled, distressed, ruined, striated, pocked, punched, kicked, peeled and peeled and peeled thrill me, things eaten away, I love to spend years behind a green rot veil, like an old bent nail, and hope the sky will one day be my mongrel suitor, be my worm dog to eat out flesh holes in me, and make me lovely. I want to be God's Clocharde and bring Him down with me. To LOVE. Love Dumps. Glory Gobholes. Glory Eatholes. Glory Eatsjoints. Glory Dumps. Recycled Midtones. Beautiful Junk. Voluptuous Leavings. Sanddune samurainesses. ShmataSamurai. Robert Rauschenberg, the Shmata Samurai of Art. The Divine Rags. Solace in Shmatas. Trash Solace.

'And the goldenness of the undercover covert overtnesses:

us, just walking around in plain view, hidden. Because they could not give a name to us, they did not see us. But we were there. Heartbroken.

'Art had reached the Promised Land; or so Art said; we were there; and so the feeling was: why not die – we are in Boom Times – But friends, I ask you this – What is a Boom Time, without War?

'And no time is darker than the Boom.

'For rooms are full of liars with that up-touristic everything is great, fine, voice, of the Boom Regime.

'(And back we went to the rants of Inner Rabe of *In the Boom Boom Room*)

'And we sailed in underground gold gnostic tunnels. We sailed in gold rooms of our own. And the gold rooms of our own were the world, we had a room of our own and it was called the Cosmos and we went out into it, we were not a witness to the headlines, we were a witness to the war, we wrote the headline, we took the pic, and they were a witness to our witness, and they wrote as if they had been a witness, and we ratted them out, looking at their books, they had been a witness to something, but they took that something and hid it away, and they used our witness articulately, but we were the Unarticulates of War; they protagonized protagonists talking like experts between dialogue quotes in ways no one who has seen a thing ever has or ever will; and no one said anything and we went apart in golden ways.

'Cradle me gently, you cobalt blue. And put coins of Charon Chlorophyll upon my eyes and bury me in a trash heap with a white shroud on, of muslin, the better to be eaten faster. And in my arrivage carriage, I came. In Fair Noir. I was looking for midnight blue parasol to shade me. Too shade for the room. Down Hip. High Hip. Thou Divine.

'Toil and tics in the summer. And these grands immobilization terrors. Rambling immobile is my want.

'Just hounding dusk like a Light Maniac down into disease which was the name of cities, I caught that Unremitting, baby, New Orleans ... from bright to night, things walked up to me, as I walked up to them and dusk came like Augustine aestivating aeva at last released; I was suspect in the fine in the lack of a thing; HERE'S A LITTLE CESARIAEVORA FOR THOSE DIGGING THEIR GRAVE IN THAT UMA BOA FOSSA *Dark* COM "BESAME MUCHO" – Kiss My Grave, Punky – I lay around in the Latitudes of Horse, & once in a while I threw a cut off: HERE'S SOME "ALL OF ME", WITH SINATRA & BEFORE THAT WE HAD US A LITTLE *"All of Me"*, with Pres and Teddy, and Wilson swings like that wildness, all calmed, in deception. So smooth, so sartorial; he could be dressed in keys. And Lester knew. And Pres was my Buddha. He knew, but he did not tell me. He waited for me to find out.

'Chances d'un vaste plateau nu au rez-de-chaussée et d'un autre au-dessus —— D'un vaste *Momma!* plateau nu *naked* ay rez-de- *give me your nose* nez de chaussée "bones of your mouse" and One Thing out of a boot and a round of a house call bet odds bones of a HouseMan not outre, just nu-dessous of Something in new volumes of fur fours of overt oven-driven sensation, disparate in our poor; to redrive the atmosphere i prorides of adventuees and be back in ancient some and ancient printing factories my desire to be my bedrooms, slow men made me fast love them, some retire, some respire, svagues, in vague segues, rouge volumes, singular sinners, Boogie-Woogie Rouge-Onge, Rouget; Dharma Toos Tushies; Lao-Tzu Tushies, it's not the in, it's the after, it's not the pain in, the alternive is where, Master Avenue.

'Poe mi maître noir, Eddie Al, I love you, Walt, my fancy-man of magic-journalism calumny nights, Mr W, without you what would I do?: Van Morrison whispered to me off the *Hymns To The Silence* tapes, off and on and on I played Doctor John's "Quality Street", and Van whispered to me in my ear as I slept,

"Tommy Street, Tommy Street, Tommy Street, Tommy Street",
and Tommy I knew he was a Marine I'm walking down the pink
rose gauntlet to the Vanguard Garden in The Rose The of it all
feel, he had them hypoglycaemic aura jitters, he had that
erethric aestivating eclampsia put a *coma* on me & that one
extra posspell syllable bugged up my jitters up onto a Marlonearse buttery, he had that mercury feel, he had that long corpse
hood shroud march into the desert mountain air of it all I see
him, he had that limo coming and you have readied the effects,
he had I am going to die joy you see shopping, faces, cut down to
essential tasking, Tommy, Tommy, he / you had that effortless
air of the soldier, at his sketchpad drawing, in extreme nowness
unbending, staying alive gutknotted inside, by forceable hand
training, and all reliving, and getting some relive here, to relive
first time I hear him falling in love with the sound in the taxicab,
jivie jasmine jumping cream mansions in a nofro cunt tree hot in
delta detriacs, on the radio, he was the sound & the recreation,
the sight *of* the sound, he induced himself into being by his desire
for me I was walking into the Garden Vanguardista in a green
black haze I was coming down the path into the Two Way Stria-
tion love is & never politics & never power but something way
out of the word intimidate the timid use to describe the contact-
timidity they bring down in others but pospolitics into way into a
human completeness so ever to say in am umbrage in an umber,
taking umber, to even say to say unandroge: just – the Destiny,
just the Tragedy, just the Ecstasy, quoting Rothko that occluded
DJ joy: that lack of melanin in my eyes may be made me night
blind by day the to the heaven – to heaven's headlights, on
brights & still I walked that Endless Nola walk into the garden,
… wasn't just to hang my hair down, hear? Honey? Ja sang in
nun knee can nigh ever tall storeys, less sign try and said, dues
you. Tall stories. You, Jess, hang, on the phone. May that honour,
with joss chording Mike or Gal, pity. Lemme read, redo a Lil
Jack, will son? Summer for, before you're.

'– Egregiously back in, joy it. Sew.

'... Sew demand, caller up. Her name? Mercy. Cyst of Mercy. Mother cyst, Momma C. tan dirty thirsty sanguine sank in thirty-seven onda.

'—— Love C.dial. 1037 on the –.

'Frequently Ma, due late it —— modulated Love Band uving you're armed, babying lap the uv swing eye bean hopping le temee tock to you-do a bit of starrying, staring some time. I'm glad you happened. Dewdrop, by now in the Dark Night of Yer So Is. Back aisle B.C. ing you and nawl family in your hunt, zone till this is Mercy on the Loooooooooove dial member nigh noose.

'A pin, too. A noffing Love Street, love's treat'll be a back in the dark kiss time to more and now wits tie further To Mudo show, here's Tommy, hey Tom you. Whata you say, U., got plenty of zip in your nada pants? Some Walken in *Deranged* & and before that some "Careener Shy", with the Blind Buddha, Ray Charles save me.'

'Hee-hee hee-hee here at the Udo Hotel we won't walk we push good afternoon – all you dengue salivasuckers, all you malarial correspondents, all you Yellow Jack strain (riders) riders, riders' spiders –,' going on in the interior of the cab,

'... 'Hee-hee – I just pushed my nothing off the landing of my hee-hee pad –,' arriving through a green mist to twist down to meet my Fate, meet Tommy the love of my life, this hepped-up Radio DJ made me want back the involvement I once had in my onces of nothing, arriving into them so quickly it could be a slow handling out through the plane's mould interstice hotting us as a.c. involuntarily iced hotties happened to nothink and hottieismos unmurky but in the in that – desiring. Into our eventualities of the rotted pot, and into the cold airport, the hot cab line, the cold cab, the radio bebop chatter, the heat coming, the mist through hot green rain like a human refrigerator, Tommy Radio's going, 'Cockroach Lounge Chair alert! Canapé

Alibinos, Hup to IT! Couch albino eggs, just them wings hatching! Fly on gossamer albino pestclouds! Suck on, love bugs enamorata du windshield smooTchjuice.... Ah.... Crotch alert, on high! Get them dental dam just broke the bank of the levee ... okay haunters and reposers, how high is the moon, how high doth thine crotch rideth and & ampersandy etceteras.

'Wake up your crotch toupee angel meats! Wake up your crotch tap dance! Savion Gloverize me to funky heaven! Wake up your crotch toupee ménage mange arrangements! Arrange a date with your crotch! Wake up that table set! [Get them fur dramatics moving!] Get them furbelows up above that datedue passementerie of some gimp amped in and put a little sweet paillette on your soul ass baby.

'Get them fur dainties to go doing you some Toupee Cha-Cha! Get them fur daintolas to go do you some coffee 30 per cent grace down your throat.' I am sweating dying. Time is of this oneness. I am the Dust and the Decomposition. Cur breath. Mother Sauce. I am an anonymous art soul. Arriving out of nowhere to a place.

'No goober, no menthol, no tee-shirt.

'Dirt Mercies. I am one of them agony souls. ST. LIP. A simple black in the agonnoose. A kin, again. Knowing why. No white neese, after Labour. Summary you came, back in homing. Then a mad man a girl say, to the alley garden, when we were sand and in and when we were sander sins in the guarding. I am one of those travelling pieces of Angel Pirate Meat, I am one of the travelling pieces of soul meat. Under fomite-laden skies. Down in early humours. In early late twentieth century days, yet. And scientific kites were sent skyward to check on the cloud disease. Crawling vermin tells the tale: tells us nothing and when literature began to present itself as scientific proof my soul left and went back to the Watch of Dreams. And to the ears of wrists and to the heart of radios going, *"... I am not the child of word scientists, I am the child of word dreams...."* "I'm going to stick all you listening mosquitoes in one big rock – rocker and roll roll chair – your what they did last night default you you walk alone. Momma you been a multioffender of my heart you are no virgin on Love Street, you are no firsttimer on thanks Momma on thanks this there then here now, there, is we wish to thank you Miss Mercy was that Lonely Alley or Court – that ever everpresent effervescent Miss Little I say swap your flood vermin for some absolutely guaranteed coming at you Assurance Alley banks down Miss Mercy, Dark Street for handing over that one single sole baton on her own today with this morning with her button on my I-wish bat on I been itching like some kind of scorned summer attack of some big Mr and Mrs Heap blue cloud with them swirly cumulus paint jobbies of white – wash – don't leave your whitewash too long in the money Launᴅ ʀyteria it might come out some coin shrunk psoriasis swam with some Kevin Spaceyed out, in *Swimming with Sharks* – did you not love the part where he's tied up and the guy cuts him all up draws paper all over him with blood for his palette, just down that Saliva Exchange Alley Cats and Exchange Meow Kitties – okay what cockroach is waiting on the hold next?...." be acts. We may be the sum of them. Let the goose hang high. Oh baby be sweet in your badass bee-wax. In the mourning sum you are burned to bees in your throating. Oh surely you are who up from your gut. In the gurb of there shone on wrys. Grubbing a sin the morning shower showed her. Flowers on down in the flowing. And thing sin indigo. Vocatrix of all islands. Decompose volumes and the whipstand branch. Escaped from cultivation, a wild alien I was to culture of the overrefined kind says degree, in time, makes it kind; but it does not they lied to you. You have to remove to the Greater Reclusion to Recuse yourself of wordly things makes kack of art of the uptown do-do kind. And to the cities overtly covert I came. Humans unintime to me, later, in time, expressed leftoutednesses that they did not know what I did, apart from them.

Arriving out of war many times to New Orleans as my Humid Desert of the stations of to-know something; love. Tudor Tommy! Yo, Sparkito! – fry me some bourgeoisie, on the geo-bourge undress! Going, "guy, … Yeah Okay funky pocky mark pok*ee* or equipaje volare Washington bye-bye your mail will forthwith the luggage or female maleta bad boy coming through on the Udo Hotel show in the glued morning borning to — you might AM nighty wheel hair Tommy and the Big You Do It,"' : …. …. In now here's a little bit for all you this a.m. in that dark itch flea agon bite watch day night here's a little 'Love Street' goes something like this in this long hot August hot wee. Way to go. Dogs walked. And I crawled to work in the long hot sick beautiful dawn, up Ursulines in this greenness. I was asleep in the mudcompact listening to the bugs. I woke in the dark. I awakened to my bodilynesses in the divine obscureness. I was in the pure word deafness of meteorological systems coming in like tongues in an ague whipped by calm to none in the use of a Thou in the subterraneanismos con fealties sin wens Wit Trays into the gardens. I was feeling Willem Dafoe climb down, in the golden, and it's all feeling Moroccan, again. That Tunis Thing. Aft a limb down off the Passion Flower, of red and the coronas in the garden, off the pink walled and into the and off the cross in the garden and off the snakegold night of fire and into the and out of that Last Tango Gold into the pink and the bounce. That terra cotta New Orleans Shutter Bounce and the nuyorkeño wex hex-nexi mad nest the trees are, come December. That August-December nest. In the loving.

Aft, a summer Tao showed her.

Cloud Tummlers, and you, often the guardia. When we were stand-ins, for the the carbon, in there, there, and you had the AND, on hand, from the fields.

Some Sleep Tumblers don't you love how some days the clouds're. Well, just are. I'm getting some sleep tummlers on in the you of a thousand in the you of a thousand subways the feels in when with rays in the guarding. After, a summer showed her. When we were standing in the car and you had the and the feels were always wet with Johnny Ray. Tommy. 'Misty' with Ray. And we watch the pulls fall to the grounding. You came back, homer. Treated to and you were roping that day, came back to being guarded. And the love was shining as you wore violent colours. Somewhere a bee was on your phase. In the God you fell. Hesitate, so silent. And we heard the churl we love so much, wens something like: as I touched your treat so lightly, in the youth of subways. Little elegant scuzzcats under the streetlights, Oh babies I have seen you enflame with organs of the light gone magic photographic in the sleights of hands we are all prone to out in the phosphor. Bourne in mad mansion I have wandered in and out of green pastures and Sam Cooke was in my purse in a matchbox radio and Sam Cooke reminded me where it is at when it is is an it's and when it's is an its, of totally possessive. And to recompose in the decomposition of the vagues of volumes, hivers to river to be flowers down rivers in the summer-August, yes. I have wished to blow you a second harp of a colon. Cloaked in my black vinyl magnificence I have spun you my Mercy as the rough cut 78 sound, I have spun you Mercy at seventy-eight revolutions per minute, in that rougher cut, thing, more like a diamond jewel shone studly of the night, rough, but 78. I woke up. The phone rang. It was the radio calling. It said, Get your a sinto work, you 'relate. I walked in the hot low sick beautiful air of dawn like Erev Paradiso, with that matchbox to my ear, listening to the Johny Udo show, but it wasn't dawn at all only the sun not rising. And Johny Udo was taking calls as the matchbox spoke about two below. Hair in a bout about the two below. John Lee 'Sonny Boy' Williamson earlier and then John Lee Hooker. Hairing about the flue. A little chunly-hookah in the Johny Udo Show was squawking like bops barked went along the lines of where was I? Oh Johny. We'll Johny later. Johny Later.

And Johny Matchbox, Johny Eager, Johnny Eager, Johnny El Guapo, Johnny Clay, Johny Udo was saying on the radio, in the hot New Orleans summer as the mists were musts with rain brain drain dreams of summer into garlic and with your violent cholera I cloaked myself in the decomposition of vague volumes of space, listening, walking to work, to the radio listening to the radio which was a matchbox which contained Sam Cooke's soul remains and Johny Udo was on the radio as I went down on Bourbon, and nearly fell into that sidewalk crater on Bourbon getting close to Ursulines to hang a left. And in that post-daddydustifying I heard the Johny Udo Show go, (IN the garlic, standing misty with the sirens [and your fingering me tipped my phase]) in my night vinyl grave, in my night walk museo, on Vinyl Avenue, past Rain Court, through Love Exchange Place heading to Love Circle and Love Cul-de-is that a sock I see there all full and, baby, cashmere, or is that a little you been thinking about Momma in that faraway hotel room in that nice wanting Lotus position, again, maybe Momma on the Radio can be your little divine unprime premortem Sock Substitute, you dreamed of –

– along the lines of the night wander to work, kind of slow rot into the atmosphere, kind of a ground mould made pretty green paper, kind of a veil all so mouldy it could have been love and emulsion, back in the background and out of the main stream and back into that first rain as my second language. First I spoke the rain, and everything came after. First I spoke taps, and my feet were my first language teacher. First I speak the syncopate. I always go the beat is off the first one. I woke and I was alive always in the on-the-one. I woke to the Primordial Funk. I was on-the-one in the womb. My little toesies came out tapping patent.

I spoke river, first. And then they told me I was human. I spoke Chemical Lane. // And I do not know how many words it takes to make a photograph. Dust me down to the Chemical

Desert, again, Lord. I been Lonely so long. I been lonely but not like this. I have been lonely but never in wartime in Peace like this one. Dust me back to the bent light, Lord. Dust me back to the blue desert Persuadings. Let me go back to Lester Young. Let me be released to the President. Take me from the Canyons of Lester, to the Mountain Marlon.

And – I have gone to a more finecut black spin of me, in vinyl, in my vinyl cloak of Mercy, in my vinyl shiny grooves have gone on from the rough 78 night v (and your finger tipped my phase) inyl, you were standing in the garlic, wet with me, and in the misty wet with sirens I spun me at 33 1/3 much more finely. More fast and fine, or more slow and rough. I been watching *Last Tango in Paris* of late. Baby, I AM your night vinyl. I am the Night Vinyl Grave. I been watching thinking of things. I am the Night Museum. Tommy, slow motion at a fast speed. I am the Night Grave spins of old past speeds, still with us. Still, with us. I am the Six Feet Under Voice of Vinyl Past. On Vinyl Avenue. I am the Ghost of Vinyl Past, never left just returned to the Sam Cooke Underground, in the Sam Cooke Background, open a secret in the Soul Wandering so night we all have implored, Lord, somebody, Save Me. Help Me. In the garlic. Daddy Dust by me some dust make it oh and yes you do and Mercy was on the radio and Mercy said: Daddy Dust by me a little UV. Buy me a little IV of a little UV Meter, wear: thrill you. I want to. By your hoarse – and white, black, in charcoal, sienna, maroon, umber the Decatur lay in the gloaming so beautiful in old-country shades. Umber, burnt umber, burnt sienna, ash, soot, and WORD lying in black night time of day regardless. In our regardlessness in useless use may we be. Tommy, I have been trying to figure out why. Why did you hang yourself? All the Sam Cooke we smoked dope to; all the movies we saw. Tommy, remember how we used to watch *Last Tango in Paris* for that *Chinatown* Syndrome: forgetting we ever saw it so we had to keep going back to *Chinatown* to see what it was about *Chinatown* which had the art to make us forget it so much so that we kept re-viewing it for the 1st time up past the dozens, amazed we'd seen it before, every time.

And it knew how to make that happen. The secret of true art is in its secrets. The secret of true art is to put a desire in you to lie down with it again, for no reason.

Peace is kept by the eros of secrets kept between the writer & the reader. When those who have not read a thing & those who have talk of what the economic political position of the writer is on such & such, ably, then art is crippled to its heart. Only when those who know a work of art intimately & those unfamiliar with it have nothing to say to each other will art be revealed back to its fold.

(And you return to these tendernesses won't let go of you....) Thought I'd re-view *Last Tango*, again.

Right may have been marching the flee right out of herein, and baby, and found that nice nudie of me, sure.

Cuvée Van – Cuvée Crib – Cuvée Criade Cuvée Mercy Cuvée my little Cuvée Valley, Cuvée Quim, Cuvée Canyon.

Any you guys sat there the lounger in that one leg under the right tush, one leg straightened out, on some high back *orange* chaise some good luck orange, say, chaise in a room of a say celadon back of the orange & on the right that pale blue blue grey very hard to find – that elusive not sky not even pale a n – almost form of white but a pale pale but pale pale pale pale not even blue – blueito on yr right, celadonlimey back of you, you on an orange chaise – & the dull blue grey mauve call it the 'Sinatra' chair – had to be orange – my best sort the feeling good luck below the legs, by the Moon – tonight. A little hanging good luck, oranges remember that Bacon painting – I mean, right there you got a good luck lounger – a sin lounge – louche-international. Let me talk you down through my premortem tango.

Look at Marlon – join me – (don't you love how those great

paintings by Francis Bacon fit the Barbieri so?) – in slow motion raise his arms like gold Bilbao 'Guggy' by gold midnight in like a *monument* – like architecture – like the architecture of *love* – like architects could do well to not do very-*well* – at – but do well to – architects could well do to see Marlon in the opening s of – anything about *Last Tango* especially, & especially in the heart's mid-May late-May, see it May 13 to May 16 – and in a May Return, in August.

The heart could do well to see Marlon Brando in *Last Tango*, as a maquette – a love maquette – a maquette of the shape of the architecture of heart, heartbroken.

Like coming down on a record matchbox, a thing black on the bottom, and on top box which we are a dot in the arms of a mountain. As if his coat were perpetual Paris winter light – & his head dusk extremis – & the turn of gold gold in the black teeth – You could be magnificent with Marlon as your model of your next mountain. That slightly rounded edge to the collar. Curved, not pointed.

The occasional moviegoer is content with the one brick-blink. The re-viewer of 100 times is secret & inarticulate. Those who find it easy to talk about what they are writing have ruined it already. How can I tell you about *Last Tango* okay best *Last Tango* viewing San José Costa Rica say what in of '83, '80–'83 – it was in Spanish. *Dubbed* in Spanish. It was in English & French – really French & English. You're hearing French & English, you're reading Spanish. Not *dubbed*, sutitulado. Who needs diversity. These are words for those making themselves tourists to world love society. These are tourist words for *us*. We have loved, in the dark, in many languages. Let me look black under a long just hitting the knee camel coat – 3 buttons on the sleeves. A literal detail. I never wanted to look like Mar – I always wanted to look like Marlon. I was the girl who loved – liked – loved Marilyn – but *my* obsession was Marlon. I wanted to be Marlon Brando. To look like him & dress like him & talk

like him – do you think my voice in the tango-register? Is
Mother your Marlon tonight?

Long grey stations of dirty stone: heaven. When Paris clouds
like northern Spain it is Heaven –
And Marlon like gold western clusters with night – Marlon
walking from the distance like a Rothko Canyon – I've walked
Paris many times – Marlon like a matte Still. Those pants, that
gold. And the thrill of how a building puts us in a kind of gold
& iron underwaternesses & and that day in many worlds on
Jules Verne Avenue. – 4 pieces. My husband which I think 2
used to have a Major Jones for Maria Schneider – he was
always, 'Romy', & I'm, 'Not Romy, Maria'. He was, 'Romy', he
was, 'Roy'. He was, 'Scheider, Roy'. He was, 'Scheider; Schneider'. I'm, 'It's Maria, with an n'.
    The mystery Gabinete the small closet apartment the eleva-
tor is, like a small balcony rising you up with net underwear
vertiginousesses, alluring & scary. Let me track you. Like tea
roses. Like a Rosé Rioja. A Cradle Cuvée. Crianza '95.
    What Brando knows how to do is *be* art.
    Be an object.
    If you don't ever, baby, want to be an object, well then you'll
never *be* Art. It will always back to you. But what about when
you're dead. Who then will there be to shepherd you, explain
you outside the explainers. Brando knew how to sit against a
radiator like a rock of Artist's Palette just there; just organ
heart-houndy. Like a gold mountain with black underneath got
up & walked & handled a wicker chair. Like he was draped
cloudy & the cloud went near to hang a cloud drape & he got to
be, by his very magnificence, a smaller gold hunch, on his semi-
haunches, be a made himself large or small with the smallest
gestures –
    Many Shapes –
    – Like a mtn answering the phone. At home with his Lucky

Little small tender lampshades for little tender long lost loves once loved & now they are over & the lampshade remains of them when you touch it.

There was such overpoliteness in the world, today, & such a nervousness of to-say-the-wrong-thing, & such a bossiness that *others* NOT say the wrong thing, that we everyone working hard to be an outsider; so nervous we had lost our athomeness, & our love, because love doesn't care. Love is a pig. A grunt. We were so afraid of Love, we didn't even want Love to Love any.

Like a meteor fucking fur before monochromatic twilight – look for that good coat with enough cashmere to give you the give if you need it, of being able to fuck a stranger without taking it off, to fall down on the floor, with her, & be that long gold marlonmtn dusk, & collapse gold, onto orange —— & weep – & have it look like despair. You want a coat to cover the fuck & look great as you put it on over your black pants your thin grey V —— a coat for real estate, a coat for fucking.

A coat which – with *one* but thin looks great —— in dying a coat makes with ————— (one daguerreotype of despair).

Friends, we have been told way too much about how love works. Maybe sex *can* lead to love – It happened to me. It happened to me with Tommy. The bourgeoisie told you that over time the very-well-done would lead to the magnificent, but it didn't. Irony over time never becomes Joy. With the right nourishing environmental factors, Irony *can* become a very well done healthy smart Ironic. But never magnificence. Never beauty. Never joy. Pick a coat which is magnificent. Which will go with a steam dropping your back when you fall to the floor fucking a stranger in an empty place each of you eyeing the apartment. Wear dark pants, a thin close fitting V, & don't forget the good shoes, the camel coat. Marlon Brando putting on a coat & taking __ seconds to do it, is an easy beater for the entire writing life production of some novelists – He was so generous, & they were so stingy. He gave us in *13* seconds of putting on a coat behind a blurry glass start a thousand, a million times more than they did with 3 or 6 or 25 books their whole life. In less time it takes to and the acknowledgements to justify the facts for their fiction in one book, Marlon in 13 literal seconds is all we ever wanted.

Marlon Brando can make buttoning a coat after a sexual encounter as much a sexual act as the act, because it is *his* buttons; Marlon can make buttoning up his coat walking out to the street a form a sexual creation more sex, in the feeling, than some guys who take 10 hours. Since when was length the question. Some guys' 10 hrs is come bla-bla. Some guys ten hrs in are like a government bureaucrat with a computer they're pounding one Sunday to make the love of their life come & come, which comes & comes & by Monday & forever after they have nothing more to do with that Love forever of their life they talked to everyone about, & pounded out of it pale, like a maniac, 12 humble dull chapters. That poor little state servant. One whole Sunday from 6 to 6. 12 full hours. 60 minutes by 12 = 720 minutes. 720 x 60 equals 7200 + 6 x 720 + 0, 12, 42, – 4320 + 7200 + 11,520 – 11,520 seconds of machine sex. No, 43,200.

In the time it takes, literally, to see *Last Tango in Paris* 6 times, a man brings a sex-machine set up by the state, paid for by the state, programmed by the state to be the same form as anybody & to have no personal handstamp —— & in the time the man goes hysterical & spends all day Sunday fucking with no handmarks, no hand feel —— in the time man who is hysterical almost paramedical in 43,200 seconds he has nothing to offer. 43,200 seconds, from one man is a zero. And another says Hi at the corner of Ursulines & on Bourbon one August first thing at the morning 8:30 to 8:40, & how long does Hi take even if like his is 9 syllables — one Hi forever you remember. That one sex Hi on the street is mighty generous. One giving Pretty Eyes.

Marlon is so giving he is a receiver –

One buttoning up of his Coat is done so attentively-offhand

it could be he is remaking love to the girl, at the door, & the coat is the proxy. That 'Marlon' Coat is making it a ménage.

That Camel makes it a trio.

That Camel's gone to a Came.

And off Sounded Street mtn. Carrying the dead world.

And after Marlon is on that cream good tone phone, why would you ever talk on an unsexy unsecret cellular. Sex guys knew cell phones suck, as far as sound. They were always breaking up. As far as security: discretion. And when the mountain phoned us, we were ____ were pre bebowered to the Mtn. We were bespoken.

If you don't give yourself up to your own obsessions, you will find that yr halfway measure, in them, will be mocked anyway, anyways, by those who never felt it.

———

Make sure that Camel Coat has a back slit.

A back vent. Because otherwise precious seconds will be wasted.

An entire sexual encounter in an empty apartment with a stranger could come to nothing if the coat has no vent.

The entire time Marlon fucked her, you could be taking off your coat off.

Marlon in clothes was much more of a magnificent model than most men – or women – naked.

What a shame to not be a sexually desired object, of *both* sexes. And how magnificent, to be one. Both the boys & the girls want to be Marlon, to have Marlon, to do for a coat – I just would, give me a call, be willing to be The Coat.

The Coat of Marlon.

That Cool 'Marlon' Coat.

The feeling new world feeling old world – that feeling Jewish not – that feeling Pres in New York – that feeling Italian-French – that feeling gold ————— that feeling spent, magnificent.

Marlon's ass, in a camel coat is more sexy than most guys'

cock, naked. Ergocoat. Night Camel. Dromedary Voleuse du Nuit. NuitDrom.

You know it is.

The question is not _____. The question is not: – anything. The question is is was what in *you* do takes __ seconds to looks at, hear, looks at, listen, see, be struck by, which is as life-changing as Marlon having sex in *clothes* in *Last Tango*. Because you are competing in that Cool Coat Competition. I would johnny another – I would rather go buy yet another copy of it, just for these *13* seconds. And thus have my mtn. Sculptors would do well to model after Marlon & Maria the Mtn. Glory one second in coats as objects of glory in desire. Design _____ You & me & the coat of the event. In the event, we were. // If you have ever been loving it in a certain light, in a light where you don't speak the language, but you speak the light, then you have the feeling, when they leave on Jules Verne Rue, Rue Jules Verne, the 1st time. Everything is nature, & new, again for the 1st time.

That mtn in Camel exuding a winter bear, that mountain in Camel moving through pillars the colour of Cafè de l'òpera, Barcelona, l'òpera. The sun Marlon can bring the sun. Rage sun without sunshine. That sun you'll never have, without Marlon. (Those old stick blinds. He had to do it by the window. That was his place. An armchair by the window. A sex by the window little glints of light to look in. He *knew* what he wanted.)

We ill took opportunities, friends, and make no returns. Guys as helpless as women. Women as brutal as men. An equilibrium of nastiness & naivety hell on record. Isn't it time to not aka a boy of 45 who exudes *naivety* regards sex.

Husband the love ague at 45, as if boys, or plumb, use Marlon, one single minute, say 13 seconds. Say one minute 20. 80 seconds.

Weenie Five Chapters, Weenie 12. 80 *seconds* of remember – that is what, lovers, we are looking for.

One place take me back to. One look & a life.
Been way swing cabbing dreams. You know. You do. Ain't it.
Think of what you do when you're lonely & useless. That
will be of use. When you feel good about yourself? That only
after leads to the noose. What you did when you were Lonely –
that is the best. I implore you. This is your Mother. Watch how
Marlon buttons his buttons. One, two & holds the third button
like a sexual remembering.

If I were a casting director all I would do is set up a blurry
architecture gloom with an iron gate around it, gold lit within &
say when a Camel Coat, came out putting it on, & outside pose &
button it, *that* would tell me if they could play a soldier, a boxer,
a Japan Asian journalist, a flophouse whorehouse small hotel
owner, a man in despair. Man I block him wore which ague 8 vets
to say, *How* do you know – doing of you who came me I and to
broach it. Man I blooming him worse in he ago 8 minutes into
say, say, *How* do you know dreaming of you who have me I used
to know it. I was a camera girl. But first came the 1st – green. I
knew. Tommy was one of – gone everybody the – the nib that
gave everybody the habitat which is fine but – nothing to do with
art work. How a man buttons his coat, honey, a *building* buttons
his horny a building reaching you at an action divine reading
you at a carton divine everything you ever wanted to know.
Nobody buttons a camel coat like Marlon Brando. This is the
rock of ages of thousands, the rock of ages of two hands, then
that standing by simple one hand & the rest – sex decline. And
the rest-sex poor nesting. Major Guys decline in full view.

Chair –

Horizontal back.
Straight Seat.
Two horizontal slats.
One with curs, the other not.
Very French.

| 152

2 Horizontal both –

& at sides – one two them

'Show'

Call for you Last Tango Chair. Calling for you ALL LOVERS.
A cream-grey turtleneck, a black jacket & pants for any-
body means looking around. Oh but, Momma – Marlon in it.
Not a Marlon, him Marlon – Marlon. The full turtle.

The burden of the beautiful.

Here is how it works:

A great work of art can be enjoyed & experienced deeply by
you at 16 & at 60 you realize you never understood a thing
about it, & see it, only now as the 1st time. If a man awoke on
Percy's Desert Island had never known about the Last Tango,
he could suffice. It would dayenu. For even if the man were
alone a life, at 80, there would be reason, tomorrow in if the
man same place. Scientists of art, by you can't agree –

They're dishing blurb – you can make my front go left, oh
don't you love how bad news and rendezvouses does that –
rhyming –

They're dishing blurb – & maybe you're the thing, blurbee,
blurb thing, go to the be that restaurant you barely have no
implants about; & then report it as being plangent & mean to …
but then there is the one you don't know why, you keep going
back to. It is the din to howdy. Theirs the are you dirt knows why
yallep gain butter to. If I sithe revenue. My treat the Marlon. If
you had never seen a film, never ever seen an actor, all actors &
all films could be known by Marlon Brando. Everyone does *not*
get a fair chance. To get up so. Forget up society. To not up so
why be that is to get up a society which is not them. Not him. It
could. If world had to world out. If world had to wild out make
of calling. Yourself. If world is freed to be fair, if world is forced
to be fair, & thus, not free, we could feel like killing ourselves.
Maybe the young are feeling it's a free world; and so: unsexy,
unhorny, uncharming, unluring, unalluring, why bother.

Long after war, when things came normally, & I'm too, I sat with an afternoon Rosé, Rioja, met the Marquesa, or was that Marquesa really a Marqués – Mother & the Marqués, Momma Mercy & the Marquesa Marquesa or Marqués so chaireyed (chaineyed) clear-eyed & saw humans I saw before I'm not kidding, & 20-30 after & coming about me could be in the seconds. And chair-eyed afternoon Rosé & saw humans I saw before I went then, & 20-30 after – & everything about me could be in these moments. Only ironic art goes stale, quickly. Real art just keeps aging, like Marlon Mtn. (Marlon Morphing.)

I was looking for the pure word stuff deafness – the blur.

I was looking for the mumble of mountains, not the articulatenesses of computers.

This has been one hour & 42 minutes, people.

– ing. The rain coming. Dogs of waterfalls ran down. In Saigon Time the green hanging occludes over the stretchers in black and white, in green. Mark Rothko carried the gurney for all of us. And I lay down on the coma bed of *White and Greens in Blue*, and I lay in that 1957 February Coma, until March insulined me, and I was back out of the sleeping of dark greens of New Orleans. And yet that distressed divine of white roughened with the blue, on the blue sky door delta blue .... ecomakayene//Close your eyes for PHOTO RADIO. Let me be your little pocket shots.

If I could tell you how I do it, why then I'd be you & not have.

———

You could do well to have Marlon be yr daguerreotype; your sun.

. Your prism, your man & the secret light, the time & the sun.

And his hand – & Marlon's mercurial Camel mtn dusk, cold in excelsius.

Who is to say that the homey sulk, the homey sulk in the corner doesn't come *after* the sex.

Who is to say love *can't* come after meeting on a street, *un*buttoning a coat, undraping it off, riding *up* in an elevator, coming in to an apt. lying down on the bare floor, weeping, two souls apart, rolling *to* each other, floorfucking, *then* standing up, then insects, then walking away & phoning each other *in* the apartment, then standing around in the note – diedown, breathing in the anticipation.

After I loved you & only then.

After we fucked, baby, I began to fall in love, with you. Tommy. Anyone who loved that daring might take a chance on me. If he would take a chance of being caught he might take a chance on Love-Me. If he gave me his all & said such things to me down in the essence of humans of talk in the Saxons, if he would be an animal of unforgiving but curing hurt by hurting me right out to get a little crying but curing hurt by haunting me right away to get a little curing, go on to Heart Prison for Life, get serious about maturing. The taste of him gave me a taste to keep coming back for more to feel the loss of him I felt from before I met him. I been scolded for filling guys into blanks of desire, baby. My God, if that is my sin for Scolding, Scold on, Dear Lord.

For I was always looking for men, for I was always Lonely. I was a Human Baby, after all. And selfesteem just didn't work because it's a condition of Perfection, & Perfection may be *Angel Street* or *Angel's Gate*, the luscious cop of the Angels, the workshop of the angels, but perfection is best left alone by humans. I was looking for something under cover, with the nerve with me to Lonely. Sex is the Mating of Lonelies letting their Lonelinesses to the euphorics.

They'll never be another Brando.

Baby, wear that Camel Coat, that grey V, them black pants perdition.

Make me know how they'll never be another; but make me know how slowly.

Give me a dark night I can *use!*

Give me something I can use to survive!

Don't leave me stranded! Tommy Nights, take me back home!

'You are, you know, pretty eyes, my *Red, Brown, and Black* to me, Mercy. Mercy: You make me a fine despair. With you a fine dark night might be possible.'

'Where the cloud boys sing.'

'Down in Two Below.'

'Cuvée Culo?'

'Si, viene El Taxi.'

'Harriet-Hut por favor.'

'Taxi Louie?'

'Si Free Louie. Frère Louie Taxi Maxi; viene.'

'Frère Louie y Jean-Louie Junto?'

'Oh si juntito clarito. Los Hermanos "L". Ya, viene. Pronto Los "L".'

'Take me to *Mt Analogue*.'

'Analogue Cab – she comes; moment.'

'Louiecab.'

'I louiecab momently – Electrocution Alley: – soon.'

'Take me from Portbou to Prades.'

'We will be going Portbou-Prade via Perpignan.'

'Pink Marble avant –'

'Si, si – Pink Marble Cab, she. Avant-Garde fill young mutes I'll you my invites us goose; very goose; very high. Here is hair-port in moments.'

'Bangkok-Boy.'

'Mr Monk.'

'Mr Louie.'

'Redwoods Radio.'

'Alchemy Cab.'

'Bluepoleradio.'

'*Autumn Rhythm* in New York.'

'The *Lavender Mist*-Hotel.'

'Come the Monk Cab.'

'Taximetermonk.'

'Mister Mountain.'

'Taxi Numero 1957.'

'Cab Whiteandgreensinblue. Oil Cab. Drive me. Bring me.'

'Oh taxi – viene?'

'Viene Ya – El Taxi to Vienito maxi –'

'Oh maxi taxi – Viene dista venista.'

'Oh si, clarito no problito, pas de way. Paws Up Cab she is coming. Marlon Taxi viene – Cuvée La-la. Cuvée Coucher si. Matarse – no prob. Prol Cab – on *his* way. Reserved Ass no – problem. We are taking you to The Dairy Case. Your lunch will be free to wonder. Si si. Vale, Vale. Vale Parking. In the Dairy case are being hair conditioning with ya. Londes! Equipaje very equipe gone is vola sin Washington. We are all dogged down. More human later today. And drew then threatens. Then! Internal hits in every bed. Singles only made a flea. Burp marmosetly & we are thanks to you.'

'Is Tango is fine you. Father's Barber's. Daddy's is Nu Close. J.J. Amor. Very Styling. Always Opened. Joy Jewels. Yes No. Joyas Hoyas Hoy no problem Oy Taxes she comes. Yellow Ice Whine I see. Hielo is the Hell of it – Resto Marlo is very exactly thank you.'

'– Viene El Nazi. Vienito Taxito, si. Ya Taxi I *here*. The taxis she is here right now 5 minutes ago soon; please you to wry les. Pleasing you to wringles.'

'Ya's Barbers' pleas nont dairy cases in thank you? Dairy's Marlon. Please not nor if your meat with Italcs. Milk & meat separate entires. Please not not drink from the ass of a mule. We all hands down then Avenue of Johanna's. I dug gold 49s to the sea.'

'Mirandize me back to Johanna.'

'Down in the quim canyon tree.'

'We present a view of your balcony.'

'Love that terrace.'

'Love that terracing of – love. Love that love-terracing.'

'I balcony, you balcony ...'

'Oh do I?'

'Ever think of Sinatra and Marlon?'

'*Guys and Dolls*, sure.'

'Who else as Maria?'

'Chet Baker?'

'Good. Nice. Remember "Chet Baker is twice the man your Momma ever was."'

'"Chet Baker is twice the girl yr Daddy ever hoped to be."'

'Chet and Mar – not bad who else.'

'Sinatra – Frank. Mr It. La Voix y El Look. The Look and The Voice. La Voz y El Mirada.'

'Marlon's both mirada and mirador.'

'At the once.'

'AND Miranda.'

'And Johanna.'

'AND the mule.'

'And the bracelet.'

'Necklace.'

'AND the necklace.'

'And the neck.'

'Neck, necklace, look, lookout and the ocean of the sea of the pacific we walk on out into, willingly volunteer 49ers to the dropoff. Just for one more glimpse of you, Marlon.

'Frank you say? Frank as Maria – wow!'

'March that flea.'

We were so much more.

We were starlight.

I was looking for a kind of Imamura *Vengeance Is Mine* night serial killer blue, 30 minutes into the night & the killing music. Yesterday I woke up after sleeping after my shifttime &

shuffling for a perfect Saturday afternoon just got up & it's 3:20 in the afternoon, I found *The Funeral* & I watched it.

Gallo is Johnny!

Johnny Coma!

Johnny Funeral.

Tommy Wheelchair.

Johnny Coma.

Johnny Coca.

Johnny Cock.

Johnny-Dew.

Johnny 'Dues',

I was looking for a good union boy – like the dead man in the Gallo *Funeral* coffin.

I always fell for Blue Collars. We were a fit. Vincent Gallo has a face I could look at from old country to new country & back to the old home country way, again. // Vincent Gallo wears clothes naturally. He's figured out. He understands the nature of a second. That he has // is being photographed 24 times. He poses while moving. He sits there collar slouched, suit in a rumple-natural letting the cigarette do the work; letting the cigarette carry. If a script with the lines right requires no more than be carried by it, then a man who knows how to smoke in the movies knows how to let the cigarette be the lines, and the timing; just as he can listen to the acoustic space of the clothes.

Like a Gallo *Funeral*. In a kind of an Egon Schiele aerial view. Perhaps Vincent Gallo may be best viewed with a waist harness hanging from a ceiling fan, to get that architectural space of evening which Schiele got in *Reclining Semi-Nude with Black Stockings* which I became Enamoured with a certain Friday in December, a certain New York Friday, a certain December Friday. Dec 19/97, viewing the gouache and pencil at Galerie St Etienne and I was put in mind of the blue back shoulder cape of the woman and the short black kind of toreador bolera aura and the black stockings with the red ribbons, like someone carefully took the typewriter ribbon off and gave the lady's legs something sexy to wear. And it looked very aerial. *As* if love, in true, always is looking down from the hanging position erotically; and Schiele always looking like aerial maquettes of New York City architecture. And *Reclining Semi-Nude —— Black Stockings* always had for me, after, the air of feeling I remembered of the shape of the Quinta Avenida 'Guggy'. Like bodies always were the architecture of museums. *Black Stockings; Rite of Spring; Black Spring; Good Blonde & Others.* Tommy, remember how we used to call each other up, just to listen to the sound over the phone of cigarettes going down. Vincent Gallo has this look of gratitude. This look of pre far gone and cover of one of my biggest regrets was maybe it *was* that, was it the same Egon December I saw the Egon Schieles at the MoMA and St Etienne, 24 W 57th St, after at Long Fine Art the Motherwell *Delta* (before Long moved to Brisketville in the first W. 14th Meat Art Vanguard – and still the Hudson construction was low, for a while & the sky horizontal & Hudson River Desert, before the Boom frilled the sky in, to Clyfford Still canyon slivers. And the cynosure of all ides). Or was it – & then I went to Coliseum & got the Rilke – and I remember not springing for that Italian VOGUE UOMO with Gallo on the cover; and ever after regretting it; because I kept thinking of his face; its loveliness; its something. I would if I could cast the world, always include a little Vincent Gallo in every movie, to keep the screen good and dishonest; what Vincent Gallo knows about posing is what the original voluptures knew. How to be sober and how to wear honey. Remember in *Buffalo 66?* Where in that club, and that strange kind of stoptime sense ... it was like an art piece. It was like a kind of rauschenbergian combination with a rothenbergian horse dilemma race and a shermanesque costume march and a milchian nypdy rough gruff and offhand wild accurate nuts inmate of the what does a man do when he is born in freedom, and knows it? Few do. It's a terrible burden to be born into

Freedom, especially if you know it. It's a painful burden. I been thinking about those typewriter-ribbon thighs of Egon Schiele's.

Spinning them eyes of Christopher Walken.

Customs.

Dogs came slow, but in a fast way.

Down Angel's Gates dogs drifted down down to *Chinatown*. *Chinatown*.

I'm the leopard with the most minkers.

The music *feels Last Tango*.

That easeful bleach. That long-ago light of pure natural resembling.

Time to roll and it's at beginning going slowly –

5 seconds, 10 seconds of distraction ——

I liked how the white suit Jack had on matched the white suit Sean Penn was wearing the night before, *Sweet and Low-down*, Jake & Emmett in twin whites.

A mixed-moment is weighed for you.

Dogs slept.

I let them lay then watering poor hounds down the sleeping dog liers. Most hardworkers can keep your interest for a portion of the 1st 1/3 of a book; the question was how to *sustain*. Sheep went to court. Shepherds will held on contempt. Dry & by the desert. *Chinatown*, accidentally. *Suddenly*, in time.

Caught between the Pacific Ocean & a dry place. Caught on rocks. There was kind of a pale air, a worked air, the rock at the Pacific cloud like horizontal Central Park offcrops & all water off Fifth & flat. A pure washed light – so pure it was hard to say – in the eyes of Jack. 10 minutes into *Chinatown* you're long hooked. You're a John Lee Hookee. Jack was lounging like a latter-day deep gold looking mountain Marlon. The sense of possibility in the play of things should never be *under*played, in allure. People made art with no respect for the pains of the materials they were at use, with. The way Nicholson wears a grey suit & the way Vincent Gallo wears a suit; both tasty, both different. Jack's a 4-button guy. Word: 'terrific'. If you wear a hat wear it like you mean it.

—

I always forget Faye Dunaway is in *Chinatown*. If I remembered ... would I see it? Then I'd remember, & not have to. Never get that repeat surprise – of Love. Higgins!
The pale play of the reservoir refractions.
The bent blue pale Desert and the pacific resist.
(And the 32 1/2 minutes in, it seems it's been going on in the good sense forever. 5 minutes, even, 10 & 12 & 14 & then 33 – Dead!
I like a body in the 1st half hour, slow but inevitable as a fuck.
I like a movie by accident, which changes your life.
Because it gives you the means to be able to see it. It shows you the means to read it. Only with its unableness can you enter its brokenness, broken. Some works of art are not meant for the able. They're in this meteorology of need key. Some things you need to be broke down partway before you see you were born to read them. Some movies need you in that light dark-mood, in a Santander kind of feeling, before you see what the man means: only his means he was desperate for are the connection for your needinesses the neediness in him superseded heals you. For an hour or two. Until you're murdered. But ain't it sweet, in the meantime.
I like chance by attention.
Flexibility is the hardest simple thing.
Role-playing doesn't work, because it's the surprise you have to play to lose the role, in life.
Built on water, built on rock.
Built on faults, built on bedrock. New York is vertical & stable. San Francisco is *Vertigo*-in-a-fault. New Orleans is horizontal on swampy. L.A. is between the ocean & the desert. How does a man drown in a desert. The pale gold orange Paris offices

of sage and sand at L.A. that Last Tango blew pale pink above. Water, gold, grey, slate, Jack like a pinstripe rock walking.

And the wood like the pale sky infused with river reflecting of the morgueness. And big aproned mountains smoking. That pale concrete sky, the land of rust, the sky drowning of parch of thirst. The gold panned bed, wood, rock, dry bones way in the sun like mountains of water not there. And like apparitional detectives humans have walked into the Desert Beds hoping for thirst. All of Paris was below like ankle sunsets. Like windows made sage – Jack like a bone with a hat, like a going bone with a brown fedora under the underbelly of a bridge where gold & a mountain walking down the grey white bone black sand like only an element of sunset – but what a sunset – but what a secret – like a walking Jack pillar like a coloured Ansel Adams like a thing *all* things & gold grey white – like Jack Nicholson walking through the giant clothes of Marlon – the grey pullover the gold coat now disassembled to etiolated wetness – the Angel Day so wet longing reflective water & dry evaporating you solid. And the ground's clothes were *As* Marlons.

And Marlon's coat was an L.A. reservoir environs. And Paris's concrete was L.A. stones. And Paris bridge light was Jack's grey pinstripe. *Man Drowns in Desert in Drought.* And all junk gold steps by interstice Paris Twilight lit unders. And sand junk gold steps by rivers once Paris Twilight lit windows. Old going eye. Old gold age. Old gold wedge. The beginning of cities looks like the end. Once you get very intimate with a thing of art you sacrifice that – that your civilianhood with it will be over. What Masters know is not how to do it. What they know is how to bear a great loss. The loss of being able to see ever again a thing like a civilian person. And the rocks crawed like beings. And the rocks crawled like breathings. And dying days had the strange backlit in the Desert of *humans* in it seeming dusk walking to you on fire like skies.

The kid looking like he's on a grey mountain on the horse.

Noses to goldfish.

Bowties.

Jack's hand on the phone. NUMEROUS DRAWINGS OF JACK'S HAND ON THE PHONE. JACK NICHOLSON HOLDING PHONE WITH BANDAGE. BANDAGE & PHONE #2. Scribble fingers look lise side-nose. Pure shape of BANDAGE AND PHONE, CHINATOWN #2 looks like bandage shape is a mountain with flight wings on right (his left) and a hand curve: like a mountain in mufti. Like a bandaged mountain. BANDAGE AND PHONE #6. Looks like cross on side and bottom of phone like puffed up infected penis. (Or boxing glove) (what did I do with all those pics I took of the ring? B & W's? [Kid Jewels at the what was the name of it Gym?] [Kid Candomblé in Bahia, by that Funeraria? Where the hills go down to the eternal rag and skin trade louche slouch there...]) BANDAGE PHONE CHINATOWN Looks like disassembled milieu of volume shapes two squares sitting on top of another, a kind of side elephant, and a long kind of balancing under thing. Piece of chin?

Final one:

(I like)

(very pure)

(almost scary of emotion)

4 fingers of Jack.

Beautiful fingers.

I never noticed his fingers before. Just gorgeous. The way he places them; uses them; they say 'Uncommon Grace'. I would say Jack Nicholson's hands hold that *Chinatown* phone, with Uncommon Mercy. 1, 2, 3, 4, and that wrist palm triangle. 'JACK NICHOLSON'S HAND, ON PHONE *Chinatown*, —— WITH BANDAGE.' *(Chinatown #13, August 20, 1995, New Orleans 5:26 p.m.)*

To know the feeling of something set inside you have to know exactly what the air is, out. The air, the time, the weather. The barometer, the temp – the Bar & Temp to get the interior right. What preceded, what will come after.

The thing between 'were you', of Nicholson to Dunaway is 1, 2, 3, 4, 5 seconds between the 'you', and the 'I', the 5 seconds went nice due to the lighting of the smoke & the inhalation.

The secret Roman Polanski knows is how to make cinema a sleeping pill. The WORD (midafternoon?) – mesmerize; – midlune?; the horizontal homeopath; the Polanski Magic Pill; the Ecru Elixir; the Ocre Orgasmo; the sensual voluptule laissez nous nu – ? – snooze; the zen lo fi chazzen du ciné ...) – the gold cigarette cases are what inside the Pulpo briefcase – I like a man who keeps ink in his wineglass.

On Location in My Heart.

Islands of Rigour.

The old ancient pale blue sea. The name nights so grey in the green gold. The morning lights so grey in the given over old.

There are no innocent questions.

The first kissing came 83 minutes in; that's nice.

A kind of dawn pale Sessions light. A light of L.A. the colour of that elusive ecru with grey with pale lemon with pale grey with a whisper of grey blue with dilute Van Gogh yellow with old sky with weathered grey which with Drags of Dregs of Smoke dragged through dawn. You can't name the light of L.A. because there is no name for it. It's got way less blue than New Orleans, but the blue is inherent. It's kind of soul struck the other way; cool in a warm. Altitude by low by ocean. Like airs of bright garage but dawn breathing. Elusive but driving yourself to the crazies. We are the Galvanized of the Jack. Les Fleurs du Marlon. The 'E' Drivers of the Gene 'Popeye' Porkpie du, du Connection-'Lester'. Left out in the rain to mordant in the garden. Pale & Optimistic like a Pessimism dilute. Hope but only in the Joyful. Like Stockton *Fat City* grit was beautiful. But not too biooteeful (but a dark true despair) just that strange blend of L.A., in January. And these L.A. neighbourhood palms. And black night with white waves & the gold in it – these hillside shingles.

The House of Sessions.

Succession into sessions. Succeeding into blowing.

[Call MA - xxxx]

[Call –]

You might want to remake *Chinatown* with who – Kevin Spacey & Uma Thurman.

1972.

1:50 in, she tells him the truth.

// Bifocals.//

I'm going downtown.

2 hrs 3 mins at Chinatown.

Are we at Love Street yet. How long has it been?

–

1976 – S'possible.

'I Can't Get Ended With You.'

And perfect things aren't perfect. The very well done has hope of being perfect, created without flaws; you need only one encounter, & never need to go back. Perfect things can be thrown out. *Masterly* things you keep going back to & you slip into the Divine Wormholes of their rabbithole weasel flaws; those things so heart-shaped they're a fit as we return to dream in a seaweed crown in a seawater tide car in a blood run white because we're always returning things of bodies and bodies are always returning us.

In everything I have been moved by, later I realized that the vision, in it, was the slow attention of the Master of the materials, which *came through*. No intro was needed, because you figured it out, for yourself. No one had to tell you, because it was true. No notes were needed, because the thing was built in & sexy. The vision was the adoration so helpless with love, it found the means, by being broken to it, in the process.

Christopher Walken. I was looking for a man who could do to words what Walken did it some coke bottle mouthpiece stop-time Time-Motion scat-bop choke-stall slow slide Vishniacy testosterone blow-up blue look study what's his face with the horses; I mean dancers, but didn't he do horses too. I was looking for a man who came in with a blowtorch, but tender. A man who took a mountain of stone, and made Walken-Serra *Snakes* out of it; who took all the energy of terrorism and used it in ways not so much Peace, but pounded the shit out of it, just offhand, just sweet, just attentive, just all-there, just: scary. I wanted men to scare me. The truth is if you love a thing, you want to kill the artist. Things came out which filled me with no particular emotion at all. I felt no regret I had been argued into that A-plus for the girl. I felt not bad at all the boy's loyalists argued me in the paper into accepting a Bplus for the boy. But the truth is if art excites you you want to kill the artist. So great is your lust for their mystery. Things came out so completely unmysterious they gave all their secrets away, before the love, which made the love just a fill in of the prestory, or they explained their mystery after which made you sour. Christopher Walken walks into lines with a balpeen in his throat. Nothing seems foreign to him, and so he seems downtown. Very Willem Dafoe. Them darkness art school, them downtown art school guys – my flavour. Them downtown guys. Always liked the downtown guys. Never much for smalltown guys. To change your art, change your altitude. Your paint will have another drip. Your air will have another lungful. If you go to the Low Ozone Zones, you will have energies of Torridicity. Udocity. Strap your art to a toilet and throw it down the stairs to the art gallery. I was lucky. Once in a while in this life I met a man going through what I did, right then. We could be in this now, together. Gill me in, gilling in the nigh on the grit-grit. Oh I would trade every condescension apprehension reprehension apprehensive prehensile untactile overactitionized way over appraised unapprised eyes-on-the-prize for one eye blink. One eyeful. Joy me in an instant. *Joy Generation.* Make me joyful, with your beat shaft eye crack inside you was the shutter outside someone walking by saw and made the street as comatic-in-the-morning, might wake and be alert by night time. Nigh on high, or what. Was opened its jalousie slit openings to close, and drift off to heart muffs high on the lam of is in the dark nether swell fur dreamy reaches where whether 'Celtic Excavation' off the *Poetic Champions Compose* tape (black with grey) is too fast, in the sleep, with the radio on to it, with it, for you, over you, as you sleep young my darling in the thing of everything a human desires to shuck off, like feathers, just in its season. And the season was off. Or it 'twere to be a no blur, maybe, if those Celts dug down to 'It Never Entered My Mind' off the Ben and Coleman stove did mightily, babies, drove drive strive to, or if 'It Never Entered My Mind' more rightly belongs more down in the pace reaches of 'Someone Like You' in the feeling. And pillows went pizza boxes. And dogs lay down under beds while humans wept on the pizza box decor plump still did not buy wonder love for it still did not longing undies more for it still did not hang indigo lure for it still did not long we high done for it was something other & the need went on as recidivistic light to the smithers & to the & the atomic Abomb shivery smitherees. And the shivery Abomb smithereen suitcases. And the suitcases of weeping rain. – where cans sped off. Where cars sped off to safety to find death in a mask. To find. Where cars sped off to safety to find death in a crash. Dogs survived and walked into blues bars. Dogs came in off the highway in an ambu and walked right into a bar shining different. And in a small desert occlusion even on the periphery of my own eyes I saw Jackie Wilson & Marvin Gaye & Lester Young & Teddy Wilson march with a lifesized matchbox carrying Sam Cooke inside down shot & killed for no reason.

And that smooth sartorial where jazz meets at the esquina of the blues, and makes of it a rincón del alma of how Jackie Wilson flings that jacket over, and twirls as if he both suicidal, and sweet; as if Jackie is swinging over his espalda some kind of nonchalanted watchfulnesses, of the Desert. As if, when we open ourselves, to love, it hurts. How can it not. Nothing ever healed they lied to you, and when you realize that, it is *them* you despise, not who hurt you. And Jackie Wilson swung and aspun down that Heart Runway, AND Marlon Brando could make a – *any* venue a Love Runway; he swings more, just *standing there*, than most men in a: Marlon Brando just standing there, doing nothing, Marlon doing gar nichts is more swung and hung than. Don't find your *voice*. Find your *body*. Your voice will follow, with the lines, direct. 'You.' 'You made me feel the universe, between the unlikelihood of you, and all your own unlikelinesses. The kingdom inherent between unlikeliness, and unlikely.' 'I.' 'I came to you in a cab like lightning in a desert and I didn't even know it was you to whom I was coming.'

'You didn't. You didn't? You. Didn't you?'

'I did know nothing. I knew nothing of you. I knew nothing, about you, what you would be, how you would come to arrive into any incarnation of low, in the sullen things of lowlife in the lo-fi brainwaves of a war vet, just north to New Orleans, and into the cab I arrived, I came to my arrival, my arrival arrived. My arrival arrived without me, in dreams, and my body followed my soul, to dreams. Tommy.' 'Mercy.' 'You?' 'I felt you coming before I even knew the whereabouts, of you. Or that there was a you, to feel the meteorology, of. To make an archaeological dig, of the sky above, to autopsy the sky, to M.E. it.'

'Oh Tommy, come back. I miss you. Come back home to radio, soon.'

'I can't. I'm here. You'll have to come to me.'

'I can't. I'm stuck here, Udo.'

'Are you?'

'Yes.'

'Maybe not. Maybe you're here, baby.'

'I think not. I don't think so. I doubt it. Serially.'

'I could feel your. I felt the. I could feel your-very-approach, through the atmosphere, like a front of raining. I heard the change-of-air, when you came down through the guardrail. Always did. In the harbour.' Out of two below, in the swing. Just ride in, on the torques. On the tour of qua?s. Doses of evenful pains, in those in those eventful pins, in brain no-reliefs. You were my Mercy gold Aleph Treble not chart signature tune of light, in music. In duns of a grey cool ice slush pond of. Down into a worming, or worsty rinsecrack in the ass trolls sweeping off to these train stations of love-gathers, down in how harbours. And these when in quality of a rust rot eat of how in the metal goes from that rust brown and get these October purples, and still the rope rots on, and into these chains of shapes and that noosebit flower. We only want, Tommy, I do. We only want. Want only. We only want small things, with tender moments. To remember, sweet. We want things, with a procession which surrounds them, in the eventuals of a day, so that one small thing, a cobalt, perhaps, a Klein view, a Klein nu? – Bleu, a thing, a colour, but in a tender time in the golden autumn parade, makes us remember it in odd moments honkers daze and in a touche of youth, touched in the subterranean sulphur Lesters going under into the Garnichts inside a taximeter with wheels on, inside a taxi's a Taxi's Meter's, and they cut his meter off and the meter was driving down Broadway. Inside I saw all atomic neon explosions, off signage. I went from that December 20 am I right to remember Orange Ghost Snow, '95 in phone booths calling you, no, I'm wrong, the *ticket*'s going to say *the 19th*, but because of the, that '95 Manhattan in December snowstorm, we storm-stayed over one night, (and so, found love, found the personal in the business, found the pleasure in the businesstime) (far from these tea parlour lies, told of us) (come back with Mother to that DOWNTOWN DAILY, THAT ORDINARY-COOL, THAT DAY-TO-DAY DOWNTOWN DOMESTIC COOL DU –– YOU, Quotidien Cool,) so we returned, unofficial even to ticketing the 20th, – if you would make for a frame for a woman, of Anytime, the official sources available, then what would you do, in regard, to my one lonely walk in the orange snow to Grand Central, alone but for cars of buried, one human swept down Mad Ave – on, that's right, the dark late aft. The snowy apt. in this real estate, of world. To that Grand Central Harmonics of the old turquoise off the booths, gone now in the reno posOysterBar – in the then-permitted signage, & in the pos, of the whispering Barcelona-oyster Tile lobster secrets, of us. In caves under trains, we harbour afternoon lovers. We humans were after noon, lovers. When it all comes down orange lamplight in the gold, by long before the number 5. Taken by light, light took me. I was a bigamist to humans, with my camera, times gone by. I have had events both clinical and human in elevators, on the horizontal. In svagues under trains, we have been afternoon lovers. And every neon and every lamplight and every snowstorm and every rainstorm-without-you, and every individual shining calligraphic light handwriting in the inside made outside, by moisture and the desire to have it in individual lightmarks of heaven, in every nightblind moment. Of how things shone, without you, when I went in. Here's some Record Rain Bootleg szen nized nizee free calligraphic PreZ, eternally PRESent tense. Hear some *Pres in the Desert.* Lord I.

Lord I been hungry so long. I been in this desert before but not this way. I been hungry in other ways but never this. I been in this desert. I been walking in this Desert so long. I been walking like a pupfish crawling on my belly unseen. They say Lord no one knows how pupfish live in the desert. They live like primitives, unseen. Let me be a little Death Valley fossil – a little fossil fish, but alive yet.

Living below levels. Living it out in caves. Let us enter the world, by removing from it. Let us go back to the radios. This is Radio Desert coming at you. *This* is the Pirate Desert and the Sand. This is Dune Radio, baby my heart so long's been windswept. I can see Lester Young in a blue bent light. Looking off over left yonder. And with the soulful periphery. Glancing all eyes.

I can see the President – and if there were – yonder. I see the Pres, up ahead. I see Pres walking to me. It's either Pres I see, or Pres.

I see his blue saxophone like a little Dufy blue violin with a mouth. I see his blue sax like a Mother Sauce of a Matisse *Red Studio* from which all light.

I see the President, in his hunger, walking.

I see Pres and his Porkpie on Porkpie Street. I see Porkpie Street get changed to Porkpie Court, that little dewlap love addition. Lord I see the eyes.

I see the eyes of the President. I nominate Lester Young for office. I elect to choose to nominate Lester Young for President of the Untitled States.

Baby, I been missing you, in all kinds of weather. Oh

——

—— not much, only every minute of every second single day.

Oh not much at all – like a valentine in the steps up to the desert A-bomb sky.

Not at all, like a valentine in the heart blues down the mirrored stair treads into Lago Walter Benjamin – not at all – like a heart on a bench on a ferry to the Eternal Algiers of Miss.

I been missing you baby – early in the morning but a lot at late midday but most in the late golden mild afternoon I dream in them golden New York falls come December and that permanent 4:40 Central Park December dusk. I nominate Lester Young, for President of the States of Permanent Crepuscule with Welts. I – oh I been missing you so, baby – early in the morning but a lot at late midday but most in the late golden mild afternoon, then the blue hour past sundown. Then when the stars come out and at mid night. Then all night, awake or asleep. But mostly always.

: ... ... At the Marlon's Where's Clu –. Draw in my shape – One Dessert Way to go – the tresses of a tonic her – some stressed out in deserts of how deep is your Tao and I was

walking down Washington and 14th, New York City, and I was
walking one day down Washington and 14th, SoBe, Miami and
had me some nice, at Charlotte's Kitchen down Washington
from Chicken Kitchen and rest in peace, Charlotte's, and had
some GENERAL CHENG'S CHICKEN by the was it Jackie Chan
or Wong Fat, no I mean Beat Ta – I mean Wong Hong, Chow
Yun Fat posters there used to be and a man came in and
ordered some KENG'S DISCIPLE DISCIPLINED CHICKEN, and
he sat down and he said to me that Hot May Night in Miami I
was but a bit of Mac's Deuce Pink Stucco Sweat Went Around
the Corner, with that TATTOO (or is it a 'TOOS'?) off on a car-
reflect across from Mac's (and that pink squat thrilling tonation
emits out, come humid thrill du – if you were born, and called
to Dusk, what do you do to survive the rest of the sun downtime
… (and kitty-cat-corner Washington that TATTOOS sign when
hard & soft and the sec neige // the sea mirage of the Doctor
Ocean heaven the sparky deflower Doctor Ocean where the
sparky dance floor – Sparky Dance (Sparky Dance Chair! Oh,
Sparky, let's Tango-Electric – Mango My Herpes!) for the
Heavenly Inline Tango Dancers) on the smooth spaces of blue
& wall white strip lines, at there a killer. Smooth spaces of blue
& wall white ship liners, at their ankles. And the man by the
Hong I mean Chow Yun Fat film chow decor came up to me off
by the Barber's where by Charlotte's BoardUp's Death's Knell's
– *Henry Akawande!* – pops, man, the Hugger! The Huggers &
the Weepers! Oliver, Oliver McCall! That's right – *Even.* I never
Even. I NEVER EVEN TOLD YOU I HAD A CRUSH ON YOU OR
ANYTHING. Where the *Even* MAKES IT. It's nothing without
that *Even.* And he said. He said. He said and the Bus Stop and
he said, 'Here's a little something more, off the, here's another
sweet cut from that THE WAY OF CHUANG TZU, with Little
Louie and the Analogues, a little something we like to call,
  ' "To know when to stop
  ' "To know when you can get no further

' "By your own action,
' "This is the right beginning!" '
... ... A little begin right off with a little of off the gold windows rolling by – a little what in the Sam Hill Cooke – I been thinking of those hotel motel – those Motel Murders –– *Motels Murder* – the Murder Hotel –– them beaten black and blue B & B's – the Kitty Kat Kill Club – the Suicide Cafe – I been thinking about those Martin Luther King – Dr King & Sam Cooke murders –– those gunshots – thinking *of* – thinking *on* – any caller got a handle about these – looking for some caller – would a matchbox hold my remains –

Just wearing my winter camel coat in the a.c. – my grey pullover V, my dark grey blue jersey pants my blue socks my oxblood loafers lying back in my matchbox – love that camel collar .... let me stare up into the dark, here at Radio Love Street, going would a match............

What in these anglosa supposes.
What-in-the-jones is that?
Jonesanglo
Jonesanglo
In describing desilc
desolc
descoke

& Los Chicago Boys
& Lose New Yorkeños
y Las Manahattatipos
– The Island
      Boys

Los Boyos
de New York
– keep yr smarts in
your pants, baby.

desolccerrados
desolcerrados
   and
old ancient
nepoabiertas
   &
repohombres
I walked like blue fur chaise. I walked like blue fluorescent. I was orde of the Desert. I was a blue clochard. Nervous, & lit the sky of glass I walked on I broke, & I walked with shards of sky undulating me brokens. I have walked with rain as my slippers through Basque rainfalls. Fallen in the Calatravas. Into gold leaf walls I walked like copper furniture. My name was 'Miranda.' I was a chair. But I was adjustable; flexible. Like blue tubing, elongated, I sat in a gold room with coat hat stand one black smudges. I went, sat, in golden rooms. I was inside the daguerreotype of Love. I was inside the gold soul daguerreotype music flips of Jackie Wilson.... Jackie —— oh Jackie Workouts. I was at that Gym – 'Jackie' Le Gym Jackie Wilson. I was boxing soul at the old ancient Soul Gym.

I was boxing at the Love-Amateur Gimnasio I was training for Love at the Jackie Wilson Gym.

And I punched out Irony with swift Love jabs

& I hit a left hook so ToBeLoved - y —— that K.O.'d at last Irony hit the mat —————————— in a long 9 space 8 count —— & Irony fell down past on-the-ropes-El Dopa posdoping, & Irony dropped like a sack of Nightshade Mishpoche Potatoes &

& like an eightcounted Emily Dash I opened a long scissor-leg slide, & I slid them long Jackie Wilson Emily Dickinson dashes.

And back from the shadows I knocked Irony out.

I was sleeping my undignified August histamine more histamine yet than lost, & I got up, clubbed & cotton battened & I walked out walked down rushed up dressed walked out walked down walked in & in the underwater sea, down the underwater steps, down the underwater chairs, down the underwater flesh, in the under water ring with all fishes there like, finally, at last, it was all blue undulations of gehryian fish at last, earwater & the water of the great salt seas did dry & there lay the bones of the giant monster fossils, & there by the giant pupfish big as salt lakes & giant salt fish bones lit by Badwater's low bad ass low fish sunsets was the blue salt metallic lit by the sun not going down but being blue blue being invaded by red & the red blood spreading. And Irony lay on the floor bleeding from its brain, & I was glad. I slid another long leg slide & I punched Irony, even down, & the sky did more Badwater breathing, bleeding from Sky's Brainbox, & I was happy. And I kicked the sky when it was down & the black went into the blue, flowing & the blue & the red mixed it up & the three dimensions shall look 2 again, as frankgehryiana of all titanium lit metallic ululations undulated the air like old bad black red velvet & that pretty violet blue dithering. Leaning, keening to a lavender knocked up by a ruby, a middle gentian knocked up by a rose, a – an old navy – & the fish the sky was which was an old close low sky whose ceiling was at sea level —— & I walked out into the Desert, to find the world again. I was driven in a salt car & I shot with my camera, unseeing. I felt the music of the salt & I shot it.

And at Badwater we stopped.

I got out.

The sky was a low ceiling.

We walked down below the sea 282 feet.

We were at the lowest place in North America.

Far off, cluckers had Fear of the Word Meadows.

And they clucked my desert trips. I said I'm going to 'The Meadows'. But I said it in Spanish.

I said I'm going to Las Vegas.

And the words 'The Meadows', in Spanish, made the fearful of difference get up on dinner table parties & squat & grow feathers & compete with cornish game horns on wide big dinner plates as big as eyes, & genteel prunes grew feathers & did a Chuck Berry chicken clucker going, 'Oh Las Vegas, Las Vegas Las Vegas Las Vegas', clucking, 'The Meadows The Meadows The Meadows', for they were afraid of the desert life, afraid of chance; panicked by getaways, monstrously genteel at getaway sexings ——

And we drove out from Las Vegas to Badwater.

We came to Death Valley, at last.

And near the Devil's Golf Course I saw I was time, with a camera. Above me, on mtn ranges, to a lookout spectator, I was from a mirador, a simple's lookoff I was Time itself, stretching in the shadows off there. I was only starlight. I was but a bit of sunset. And Time's Hand stopped. All of the above came as a surprise to me — (Asleep still) Sitting here cutting I was but a bit of sunset

---

And at Badwater I shot Irony who had died, & I shot the posmort of Ironic. I shot — I had made a living Autopsy of Irony, & now I gladly shot the crime scene I had created. I was the criminal & the crime reporter. I was the crime perp & I shot my skell sky. At last. I was the peeper & the perper. I was the – I *am* the Perp. The world made a crime of sky & I shot it. The world made joy this crime we want & I could but only be a Criminal of Joy, at last. I went out, driven by my long Salt Limo, & driven by my salt chauffeur. I was the passenger of salt. Salt & the low places were my transport.

I was driven to Badwater, & I got out. While I shot, the salt, the Long Salt Limousine dissolved, & crumbled. My transport was premortems of my joyful transport to other things & I was heat sweating out salt into heat sweating back salt on me, &

world *Was* without Fronteras; world was wet or dry —— & Jackie Wilson came holding Sam Cooke's hand – & Jackie Wilson brought Sam to me, & down flew Lester. & Van Morrison Lept Lester in Yclept & Lovely. /// And there was some kind of a jam of love I am pressed to remember. And love in the dying filled the air, like the end of things made red sky & the sun going down like masterworks & painters. And I said, Sam this match*box* not book this box, & I said Sam this matchbox has such a high & beautiful fish red & blue ceiling. And Sam said & Sam Cooke balmed me & Sam Cooke said to me in the Desert, 'Everything's going to be all right,' & I believed him. For in every Sam-Cooke all right was the knowledge he'd been shot for nothing. And I said Sam it's going to be all right, too. And Lester was off doing something Eyeful with pupfish, in hidden places of old-war fossils. And Jackie was *as* a sun, to us, as a saltaria, at last, in our own seasonless beholding.

And Irony died all over us like low coming down *Scarface* ceiling getting into the *Taxi Driver/ Txai* Milton Nascimento Free Libre Lliure Homage to Catatonia long tall low blood drippings. And red ruled the world. And blue was the Samurai Warrior held back. And red rushed pouring & emptied. And blue held back, full. And red rushed into blue, & there was no more red, & the Blues were full again, & triumphant.

And fish spawned us.

And fish came down & the sky was a hat.

The sky was so low that day it was a dark blue ceiling red blue fish TOUPEE.

And we went out like manhole cover strutters wearing our Frank Gehry titanium fish hats. We wore bridges like head-dresses. We dressed all-dress so the sky could look down on us, & be jealous. And little dogs walked, like salt got up & perky. And dogs tiptoed like wellheeled salt. Like trained salt, dog salt got up & ran & our eyes followed running salt dogs running off — in bullet sun, trying to catch sunballs.

And it was all beautiful, & darkness.

SPACE?

We were in the dark, at last.
We were in the dark, at the start.
For if there were –
And there is –
And if there were Love, it might be.

And in the dark in the prebirth we heard in the darkness of the Desert, where there had never been light before as yet, in the dark as we walked not blind because we had never seen, in the dark, in the mountainous & shapely dark we felt by our skin acoustics; in the dark in the First Light Deafness, in the First Pure Light Deafness when all shape is that subaudition – in the dark, for the 1st time.

And in the dark in the Desert for the 1st time Lester Young played 'Prisoner of Love', & we tilted our ears which were not found yet.

And the evolutionary reason our ears began to grow was they *needed* them bad, so bad.

They needed need more than they needed Love. For Love was everything before Streets.

And Streets began in human evolutionary living, because humans needed a place to repose together, in the salty.

Humans had a need for Heart.

And Irony kept in its last rags of dying. Irony is this prehensile thing we don't need anymore, but Love was the beginning of Creation.

And Streets were sketched in the sand.
And streets were laid out in the salt.
And blobs of flesh grew ears like summer trumpets.
And flesh lymph grew branches.
And flesh grew ears to hear better Brother Lester.

And ears came to be in the Desert.

And we heard Lester Young, & it all began. Together, after to hear Van Morrison singing, 'And Sam Cooke was on the radio, ... "You Send Me"', and baby Sam himself, Sam, give it all up for – Ladies & Gentlemen our Desert Pirate, on our Pirate Suitcase, we opened the briefcase of salt, & inside it shone a gold.

And the gold thing, the gold shining thing inside the suitcase of Love was a daguerreotype of Sam Cooke. It was a premortem of love. It was sound, in the gold. It was so old but gold-fresh. It was gold & it was Mercury & in 19 & 5_ They & at Mercury Nevada I passed by the test site, & I went out into the Desert where they had tested atomics.

And in '63 –

& Sam Cooke was always going to be on the radio of our hearts & Ladies & Gents, here's something for all you boys who died in Vietnam, but you might have been in Miami a certain Saturday Night long ago you might recall-well & remember, you might remember Sam Cooke at the Harlem Square Club, Miami back-in-the-day singing here now here's a little – for all you boys in your little matchboxes now, reposing — here's some Sam Cooke......

I been trying so long to draw you the shape of my lostness.

And I saw visions of Tom Zé far brass mtn clockworks' gold defectives' splendours, inside Dale Chihuly blown opal cobalt scarlet along original lines, along unguent blurs, of sand, begging, hanging like glass chandelier giggles of the Matings, of the Marlons, of the Mountains of Soul, of the *Masters* of Soul, of the Masters, in soul; I saw Chihuly marry Chillida, & make things *made*, of the elements. And glass ahead my hum. And glass created my hair. And glass combed my hair & my hair was a sculpture, rusted in northern dark light, & we loved, eternally, & ever. We were *made* respectful of the Art, & the Solo.

Avery seaweed with the when you MoMA in hang a left when

you with the coats there, the old Dorset from the sculpture garden, sex nesting impulses to be in the Beverly Turquoise, in the
snow, all these things are gone, the snow remains.

'Ultimate Tango.' 'Vanguard Van.' 'Protagonizing the Rain.'
Soon and idly dying, sorting our confidentialities, our outs,
deserts refull with longings, go down and tidely, fit and cut, on
Day Noir Street, Saint Noir, Black Day, 'Black Day', *Black Day*,
I mean let me aujourd'hui Thee, let snow be let like little ass
étoiles, send me, down, cast me, make of me your gold shape,
make me your teeth, dirty tender tables, moors of the hivers,
rive me, I am parched, Lord, baby, let it rain, and you, I remember you, I cut you up and reput you, I took all toile and
tulle and shining things pleased me, I wanted to do to do, with
words, what light does to satin, need me I'll be your *Madame
Satan* or your Widow Dimanche with my paradisiacal horn, let
me do to you what folds do to mountains, marlonearse à toi, à
tu, let me tutuearse, be your tutoyeuse, let me tutoyer you how
sheers tutear the rain, let me make for you, a winter of your
soothing in these migraines, let me tutear thee, on up into a
tutuar until my words are as TATUAJES sign of sound tattoos,
stoops, pulls, little dog pushes, pishers, pushers, dismember-
ship applications, the application of your love juice, we Jews
getting binxbollingische flashes off each other, corner of says OY
and UR never saying, pols in the political junkdom, the cosmos
was my polis, I was a cit of the heart of Mojo Rain, sex acts
looking out windows, standing, you yourself remember these
things, and in them, the great desire for it and the view off there
of walled gardens and touristic pedestrians below, unknowing
but feeling the fuck above. And its elemental emanation coming out like comatic preeclampsia clamping their gut to the
thing and things tiny and off like giants staring out over parks
and everything tiny and humorous like giants and talking, and
SAN JUAN DE LA HELP ME! Madre Dimanche.

'Yup…? Give me your rabbit. Go!'

'*I'm going to kill you.*'

'I thought that was the way.'

'*But first I'm going to kill me.*'

'That's my boy.'

'*I want to die, since my wife died.*'

'I know the feeling. So die.'

'*You don't have any feeling.*'

'I have a lot feeling. My man Tommy killed himself, too, you know. You know.'

'*But you're still living.*'

'Maybe. Maybe not. Who knows. It's August in New Orleans, talk to me at Twelfth Night.'

'*I'm not going to be here.*'

'Good for you. Independence. Show me the way.'

'*Mother I want to die.*'

'Don't ask me to help you. I'm keeping my hands clean. I'm keeping my hands out. Mother is here to teach you to do it, on your own. Solo, no net. Solo, no hands look Ma? You dig what I'm....?'

'*Yeah. You're saying you won't kill me, for me.*'

'No way. Live, live. Die, die. It's in your hands, thus far.'

'*Would you marry me?*'

'No.'

'*Would you refuse my hand in marriage.*'

'Absolutely. Go way.'

'*But you said you loved me.*'

'No, I didn't.'

'*You he ... I heard you on air. You said it.*'

'Maybe. You have a tape.'

'*Well, no.*'

'Then talk to me later of forensics. You do it, do it. There he goes, folks. He just shot himself. He made me watch through his open shutter. He's just slumped out that window frame. Any other takers? The radio which dies alone, one by one. The radio which kills off its listenership. But only if you wish; and only on your own.' Come on home to Mommy, boys and girls ... let me love you ... vocatrix of emotion ... be like cold grey winter Paris....

After Marlon....

After Marlon Brando no one can ever wear a Camel winter coat again, in winter.

– The final possez has been filmed edited held & written. Because Love. Because he's here. Zen Marlon. Because every gesture is the lie *they* were present. Because every thing radiates its expansion of time. Because time changes, in love. And unless time changes in art's arms, all it has as resources is to explain time to you again, as metaphor, which Marlon never does: he is time itself, brought to us in a light miracle.

The dead Marlon be bedecked in ochre cashmere will always be much more of a sexual object, than a live I'm sorry to say it – you know the gig, because like Sinatra there's the True Way, the Time Why, the There Cut and the weakness of politics becomes apparent without the lusting. And when political junkies become bureaucrats, where is the Marlon? WHERE'S THE MARLON???!!! Where's the butter? Where's the milk? Where's the Marlon-Dairy-of-It-All?!

Last Peeping Hire in Paris. Everything I know about words the light of the red in *Peeping Tom* taught me.

A dark day with you in iron going out into would smatchboxes Sam Cooke the great what in the Sam Cooke and would at the I always forget the Square, sugaring me off winching ways to go yet; be let. Let me.

And in '63 – ...... coming to you, from matchbox radio, from r – Radio Matchbox ... looking up, in the dark, in my matchbox coffin, listening to MY PET MATCHBOX RADIO SAYING, 'Now as we go out here a little Sam Cooke with "Everything's Going to Be All Right", like untitled destitution of our hearts like Untitled Vietnam Heartbreak.' Standing busted at the fine....

But nearly always mostly in the Blue Hour, & in the Magic Martians' dusk & as dogs came fast but in a baffled to me. As dogs came fast but in a ballad to me.

Yours, Miss Mercy of the Night.

I feel a fit of the Preses coming on. I feel them Preses like water-in-the-desert, all night. I feel Lester Young du Pork Pie Divine coming, walking like a bush aflame, like a flathat on fire of pies of feet walking like dogs of sand. Like dogs were buts, and perros walked peros in the night. Like for all the world and pinking as the sun makes a pink of everything in this studio, why, after all-night, and into the morning and then all aft, and on which is shuttered closed and white that sun is bouncing that baby terra cotta out there in & that terra cotta of next door is breaking and entering my jalousies & even God is jealous of how pretty my jalousies look in the beginning-dusky, why they even look like white dogs waiting to be pinked.

Lord I see Lester in the Desert. If there were love, it must be Pres.

If there – & there is ___ if there were love it might be Lester Young & it is.

If there were human love, as bent light it might be the ghost of the President; he never died yet. I'm broadcasting to all you dead folks. This is Radio Grave. This is WSix feet under – this is love out of Natural Love Radio. I am coming to you on them Natural Radio Waves for long before we caught on to or to cotton to inventing it the Cloud had made Radio for us already. We are, even in the vanguard, behind the Cloud. We are in the way of things but we are allowed to pardon ourselves. Incarcerated in our Prison of Love. We are love & if there were Lester. If & it is.

Dogs in ochre overcoats walked into blues bars, & ordered a Tango. Dogs walked their hair & walked lonely in in Vuncles, in

Viets, & went in to use the john.

Lonely, but reliquyed, lonely but relieved, beaned whys, been only, even only. Lonely, but relieved, healed only in the moment, but relieved & fully in touch; lonely but relieved healed only in the moment but relieved and fully in touch with the human sex, that being human, dogs would like lepposh walked like lampposts they had sidled up to & sucked off the sulphur & dogs *shone*.

Like hieroglyphic splendour of signage.

Like hieroglyphic splendour of signs' rain detritus dogs in their uppersent dog ladders to boho. Of signs' rain detritus on their uppers went down ladders to boho, & walked into a bar, all alone, to keep that lonely BAR sign, company. BARS asked for dogs & past bond at and past burned out PARKS & quiet Vest-Pockets dogs walked, leaving BARS went all old curvy pre-neon as so forth. Like hieroglyphic splendour of signs' rain detritus dogs on their uppers went down ladders to boho, and walked into a bar all alone to keep that lonely BAR sign company. BARS asked for dogs & past burned-out PARKS & quiet Vest-Pockets dogs walked, hearing BARS etched old curvy pre-neon ask for them.

Dogs walked into blues bars and ordered a drink. Fur lay on the floor. The world was blue fur droppings. The world was fur on the floor and peanut shells from 'Salt Peanuts'. We were worthy constituents of God.

We were prisoners of lonely.

Down above streets one white albino *woof with red wolf eyes* crawled like concrete itself, bleached and helpless and vicious and growly. Houses sat like mauve graves. Houses sat like pink woof-woofs. Houses sat like yellow sunshine. I used to like to sit and look down Dumaine at how the beiges and tans and whites with a white other something and stiff and blues so pale they could have been pure white but weren't sat beside the albino other and houses were each other's paint applause. And houses were each other's paint appliance. And streets were cottage paint portmanteaus. Paintportmanteaus. Cottagepaint. They could have been pure white but they weren't which sat beside each other and were each other's port-of-pleasure. The inside and the outside. The inside lay so close to the outside down streets, I could hear the jalousies moaning. I could hear the jalousies' moaning. The jalousies were calling each other through their slits and stoops sat like throne pianos. I walked like arthritis through it all. I walked like an arthritic sun past dogs just splayed open on a stoop with a cigarette on — with a cigarette *out* on a or but the stoop side – the blue. Coffee. Dogs sat with legs crossed, out a bit on a bit of stoop with blue coffee. I walked in areas of arthritis past them all. I was dead or alive and it didn't seem to make a blind bit of difference. It didn't matter even (if) I was blind. I didn't care if heart saw me or if God despised me, or shone down His Mercy on my bones. I walked like claws but I walked. I walked like auras of preraining. I was in the anterain, and the posrain, of it all. I had been in the bellum. I had been in the bella. I had seen the bella in the bellum and the fair anglosajones much like sweet little plum hangy downy cojones in the Latinate of it all. Balls, sweet – meats and ink's desirings.

Pages walked into blue shows and added a drink. Fur layered the floor. The world was blue, for dropins. The world, as for on the floor and peeing of shills, – went *wens* of desire, yet, where from salt pirouettes as well as Pernods, salty and nodding off we are our own thing, cons, tit verbs of God, who knows. We were the unworthy, though constituents, yet, – of lonely. We were prisoners of wartime. Down above shit one white albino probono woof with red wolf eyes crawed like *and* creating itself. I am carrying a torch. Like a creosote, blech and helpless and viscous and gracey. You know, pride called itself grace. It does. But you know. But grace is only there, when you leave the dance and let the stage dance. Sprung in advance to reverberate in that partnership rooms have with sounds, if you make it – love you. Like pink woof events. Horses sat like pink wolf whys. Horses lay like brave graces. Horses' heads sat like lined-up absence, itself. Horses' heads sat in heat, outlining the border between asphalt and lower asphalt. Horses' heads sat in blue-eyed grasses' turf feet. Horses' heads down the street of nuns wanted their feet wet. In the posorris I have smelled that lavender fragrance of your love acorns. Across old lily turf and the south dreaming of having that chill bite to set off lilies-of-the-valley. The spring north bells exploding when the chill bites their bulbs off and sets them into them occasional northern spring green hallelujah fronds, and the little sweet variegated hallelujah grasses. Dreaming of steam trips of violets' fragrance in old northern woods, and the blue paint spreads of old blue scillas. Still, bleached and helpless, like a bone still alive, baby, this is Mother's Bones talking to you. I am broadcasting, here, alone, on a chaise, with a mike, in a room, because there is no other world, now, but this loneliness, and I do not know any other way to be but a Private Pirate. This is Your Mother. Your Mother's a pirate Now, on the – old – Pirate —— Wavelength. I been spinning my Platters of the Loneliness of Pirates, out to you, on Radio Natural Wavelengths. This is Natural Radio coming to you on the old ancient. Before there was radio, there were always radio waves, this is Original Wave Loving. Radio – Love. Listen to me: I have been photographing my own pre posmortem. And broadcasting my love, I hope you find.

I've been warped in my own woof, baby, from too much wartime, growling kind of Germanic, and ammo dreams have haunted me, and I have been that warning dog barking ammo at the dream tunnel, and still I loved you, and still I shot you, even when you died in front of my eyes, I shot you pre and posmortem, because I loved you, and because I loved you, I had no choice. Anglo-Saxon streets received Latin sways, and the world did miscegenate, without our instructions.

— Hunk trucks thundered old buckles and wondrous large vehicles ambled as if all short streets were cobblestones in a Mance Lipscomb kind of lust of a comb, to be blown, in old verdigris grease, of ceilings makes a good sound baffle of an old cigar club. Kind of feeling. I saw walls work blue for the pleasure of it, and crumble. I saw walls work blue, for the kick. I saw bread get lost, and brains lose themself, and rain go dump themselves in French drains, for the enormous loss of the flood-of-it-all, and I dreamed of that strange hurricane light which is green before it comes and the streets of New Orleans are empty, and I felt strange empty green-dream pre-hurricane scenes down in the ozone, and I felt joy. I could breathe. And only to breathe seemed some kind of miracle, old days past I felt, listening to Jackie. And Jackie Wilson sang, old days, the radio, — and Jackie Wilson sang 'To Be Loved', and Charles Brown sang 'Save Your Love for Me', and Bobby Bland sang 'I Pity the Fool', and Sam Cooke at the Harlem Square Club, 1963 — Miami-Vietnam days, sang 'Bring It On Home to Me', and Van Morrison sang 'Lonely Avenue' and 'Too Long in Exile', and I walked out down the off-muzette bent-tuned stairways and I flew off Lonely Street from the throne stoops and the sky came down on the river, to love me. And the sky said to me, This ain't no autobiography, baby. This is love, in the act. And I said to the sky, Let me love you, and the sky did. And I deserted the sky, and fell in love with another sky. Friends, the sky was Lonely, and I flew from New Orleans to New York City feeling like a Desert Child in another kind of canyon(ing).

And Walt Whitman stole a lick from Jackie Wilson.

And Walt and Jackie sang arias in space.

And Melville called to tall ships, 'Marvin, Marvin, Marvin.'

And I saw Herman Melville and Marvin Gaye in an elevator in New York City in some kind of water-release.

And outside the echo chambers of streets were filled with

Jackie Wilson, everywhere I walked.

I saw Jackie Wilson in the canyons of New York. And in a Manahatta Moment, Jackie Wilson appeared to me, like concrete sand on 43rd. On East 43rd I saw the soul of Jackie. And Jackie sang 'TO BE LOVED' down the East Forty-third Valley and up onto the windows of Grand Central.

And Jackie Wilson sang 'TO BE LOVED' up from the corner, there of Mezz Seating and the church bookstore and where the Captain in his office chair used to hang, and that pizza place and Jackie Wilson sang 'TO BE LOVED' to Miss Chrysler, in an aria, and Miss Chrysler on that rainy miraculous drought-ending night, did swing.

And down from the upper tiara reaches Miss Chrysler sang down white rain, from her Coma Club.

And the night sang rain of white sand tiaras rang sand of foam flowers of all eventful enfoldings, of song, we too, have been loved, in odd moments.

(And like a brave coast worth the growling rocks to switchback a whiplash of the heart from it was as if a sleepwalking summer Homage to Catatonia did, momentarily reign, in the furnace of subway track prison cells of crowds herded in, and the air above, up the stairs and that sense the diner sang.)

And Jackie Wilson sang 'TO BE LOVED' in a tender aria, in arian tenders down over the hardshell yellow ribbons flying down, downtown, under white neon Chrysler rain, and Jackie Wilson sang. And Jackie Wilson sang to Miss Chrysler things I had been trying so hard to sing, myself, with my night swinging camera. And Jackie Wilson showed me the way. I shot without looking.

I shot the night as if I were conducting it, with film in my camera, and available neon and dayfilm, by night, and using my body to swing.

And Jackie Wilson sang 'TO BE LOVED' down the Valley of 43rd, East 43rd and then I was East 41st and that steeper valley and down that Valley of East 41st which crosses the Valley of Third onto Second, Jackie Wilson sang *'To Be Loved'* down to the banner of the Library. And it was the Dead Sea Scrolls were on. And I went in and saw them. They were beautiful. They were us. They were parchment. And I felt Jackie Wilson behind me, like some kind of wonderful miracle, when you're lonely, in that special heartful way, you are, you get, looking at an art exhibit you adore, but alone. And Lonely.

With the precision of a psycho, and the vigilance of a lover, I watched the look of the sound, of things. When I felt good about myself, I never saw it. Light was music, but only incarnate if you shot it.

And Jackie Wilson came with me like my soul guardian, to accompany me with his song. He was my lamppost, he was my light.

And Jackie Wilson sang *'To Be Loved'*, and I felt proud of something other than me I could not own.

And Jackie Wilson sang 'To Be Loved' and every human who called R & B and soul 'Popular Culture'....? – well, I put a spell, on them. And they were bad luck. And they are, and they were, and yes it is. And Jackie Wilson sang 'To Be Loved' to all the homeless. And Jackie Wilson sang 'To Be Loved' to all the destitute. And Jackie Wilson sang 'To Be Loved' to all those who had been dropped from planes, at the orders of the generals. And Jackie Wilson sang 'To Be Loved' to all those herded from the ecumenical lee carton boxes, bothering nobody. On the street. And Jackie Wilson sang to be loved to that elevator which flew. And I saw an elevator fly in July, of 19 and 98. I saw an elevator up and fly across the street. I saw an elevator just hop. I saw an elevator walk that footloose creepy vertiginous walk, and I saw that elevator bop, and elevators flew, and dogs walked in amazement, and shot them. And I saw an elevator fly across West 44th, break in, across the street, land in the apartment that elevator B & E'd in, and I saw that elevator home invade.

I saw that elevator decide to cross the street and elevators flew in New York City, and humans began to predict that elevators might fly, as I worked on the pics of the lonely elevator in my eternity darkroom and Jackie Wilson sang 'Lonely Teardrops,' for the soul of the woman on whom the elevator landed, and killed, in her apartment, quiet. And dogs – and still, *dogs walked.* Still dogs broke into blues bars at night, and played bass, illicit. Dogs made art, and humans made ideology, and sometimes they switched. In boomerang collar whiplash, I have loved you.

And Lester Young blew soul into those who wanted to clean up the streets they had never been to, and the bars they never did visit. Humans wanted to feel secure about the bars, when they locked themselves inside their prisons of gentility at night. And Lester was soft, but sneaky. He was Love; and so he didn't go out *to* them. He just was: and if they missed him it was because they never came out, in a street, in a night, in a lamp-post with a dog, looking. Chance might have been there, in that sculptural smoke, looking blue, looking pretty.

I saw Lester Young on the river sailing in a blue bent light. I saw him sail up the East River of New York City, I saw him sail up that tidal basin of the ocean they call a river, familiar. I saw his blue saxophone like a little Dufy 24-HOUR LIQUOR AND DELI MEZZSAT blue violin with a mouth, alight. I saw Lester Young's blue sax on Second Avenue like a Mother Sauce of a Matisse *Red Studio* from which all light. I saw the President, in his hunger, walking. I saw him walking, to serenade Miss Chrysler at Second and East 43rd, keeping that nice intimate distance. And Jackie Wilson emerged. And they were my candidates for the offices of the moon. And they were the President and the Vice-President, of Dusktime.

And Pres said to Jackie Wilson, Oh Lady-Jackie, baby, I been missing you, in all kinds of weather.

And Jackie Wilson sang:

In the indigo of intention; in the indigo, thing of Pres, in the cooful indigo rings and the blue desert, I was a pretty little dust storm of powdered indigo, in the afternoon anthromon afterrun of blue poor, in the afternoon of blue pain, of water at last. *Oh Let It Rain!*

– If indigo were intention, it might be Lester.

– If indigo were intention it might be Pres.

– If indigo rang, and indigo couped, & indigo cooed & blue indigo of the desert blew, we might be covered by a pretty little dust storm. We might be indigo. We might be blue dust. We might be blue powder with water.

We might be powdered indigo, at last. Please, I have been praying for rain to let the sky. Lord, rain is like sleep. Lord, how the rain is like sleeping. Lord, how the rain is like sleeping all come those great grey afternoons you wake up all wet & blue & dusted-in-the —— human. Lord, rain is like sleep some grey afternoons you wake up blue & dusty. Lord, rain is like sleep out of sheep, and into the indigo at last. Loving the love.

I hear someone buzzing up the line. If there were Lester. I been dreaming of love so long. I do declare my custom to dream of love both day and night-afternoon. I see the President of Love walking towards me. He knows what I knew – I see it in his indigo pace.

Despite the blue of the blue of his face I see his indigo posture by the tilt of his flat hat – in this big blue wash. If there were love, & there is. And in war, most certainly. If there were human heart it might be Lester.

If there were human heart, it might be Pres.

Heart and forgiving of other hearts, – and prone to – but knowing always it was never his or any, to forgive us; or anybody, at all. Not us.

If there were love, in war, knowing the consequence, it might be Lester Young the President of War in Love. If there were things, a secret I might tell you, if you come close and in this

Vanity Desert, let us love on the airwaves. If there were radios which were spies in rooms & as eyeful as a genehackmaniac in flocked – it might be me: I am the eyes of this radio, watching you now. If there were & there is, Lord. And in rain. And, of course. If there were love in war, it might be Lester Young – knowing it is not ours to Forgive. Love, in the love, for you. For you, and for you, and for you & for you & only-for-you, & nobody else.

   – If there were human – heart – it might be Lester if there were human love. If there were human heart, it might be Pres. Heart unforgiving in its own forgive, because it is not up to *us* to forgive. If there were love, in war, knowing the consequence,— because there is always *war* in love theatres, – it might be Lester Young the President of Chance. If there were things, a secret I might tell you, –

   – I left 'communication' to die like a vagrant. – I confess I abandoned 'togethernesses' to be cold, and workless. I moulted feeling-good, I confess, about-*myself,* and I stomped my own old esteem until I stomped it back to loneliness.

   I began like a workless hairless myself and cold in the street to esteem *others.* I began to esteem the Big Dirty Ugly Grey Rothko Black Sky, I confess.

   I was locked in the Freedom Room of Lester, and dogs walked. Up stoops into harp teeth blue fur dogs walked and the street was a bent harp blues of blue fur arthritis. Bent prodomes of heart walked, and dogs big as buildings walked anatomical hearts, on a leash. And still, Lester, I loved you. I loved your air, your breath. And still I sat as I have always sat, down by rivers, watching ferries cross, Camden-Philly-T.O.-the Island-I watched the Algiers ferry cross by the Aquarium, and I breathed your old New Orleans-Algiers breath.

   [And I was a dog. A big old dog.

   I dreamed of looking up skirts which wound, and lifted, and wounds went straight up, in that kind of summer waxwhite limewhite upfright lemon white scalloped flight flew flying thing skirt – wind does.

I dozed.

I was a dog in the reveries of transcendence, of transferences, non-interference on the – love waves, of transubstantiation dog stops aboveground, of subways, where heat pulled into the platform and was its own breeze, in the glow of the dark from the rivers above, in the moon and the barometer rising.

I wanted the spontaneous, the impulse, the overheard, the offhand, the needy, the wanting, the hunger ships which have come to us above the sunset chimneys how to make our emotion technical.

Scraps of dreams, we are. (I was.) I was a dog.

Like wind, taught, I sat.

I sat, wind.

I sat like a Samurai. I sat still as stone. I sat for years. I did nothing. I dreamed. I shot. I took my camera out for a walk, and I let my camera run, without me. I waited for slight thrills, in enormity. Nothing would happen, and nothing – nothing *had* happened, and nothing would ever happen. Chazen enough for me was Lester's sax. I chuzzed it.]

For if there were, and it's always been true, for me. If there were & there is. Lord. In the desert the word indigo is a true thing. It is its own incarnate. And I walked out into the desert where it was *indigo*, where it was still reigned *scarlet*, where there was *frankincense*, where a bush was aflame and its name was Prez, and a flame blew the desert. I was a Prisoner of Air, dead and recomposing. A Prisoner of Breath. And the rain was my refreshment. And in rain. And, of course. And in the flaw course of it. Seeking mistakes, to be human. If there were love in the art wars, it might be Lester Young – knowing it is not ours to Forgive, but to re-fill. 'Til we rest full in the shape of our own personal nada, but raining, so pretty. Lord rain is like sleep out of sheep, and into the indigo pockmarks, at last. If there could possibly be love, and there can, but you have to be broken to be a receiver. And in war, most certainly. It is.

If in the curtains of dooms there were love, would it not be Pres? Would it not be some kind of something wonderful. Lord I been lonely so long. Would it not be the excellent future? Would it not be here, right now? Would not every breath be the one chance, of love, in the atmospherics?

(– unforgiving, but alive – working blue for the kick.)

[(released to the desert)

(dream fur)

(in a coma club)]

(And dream fur inked us)

(bond in our lunglight)

(not forging, but breathing)

—— the thing about Bertolucci is

Acknowledgements

The author gratefully acknowledges the help of the Ontario Arts Council.

A portion of Chapter One appeared in *Exile* magazine, March, 2000.

SHELLY GRIMSON

Before she began writing fiction, Susan Perly was a radio producer at CBC in Halifax and Toronto. In the early '80s her *Letters from Latin America* for Peter Gzowski's 'Morningside' reported from locales such as El Salvador, Guatemala and Chiapas. During the Iran-Iraq war she broadcast *Letters from Baghdad*. She also produced many documentaries for 'Sunday Morning' during that time.

Perly's short story 'Jesus and the Toucan' won second prize in the CBC Literary Competition in 1988 and was dramatized with Don Francks. Her stories have appeared in *Impulse, Friction* I and 2, and in the anthology *Hard Times*, where her story, '1956: an excerpt', on Thelonious Monk and Glenn Gould began her fiction writing using jazz as both subject and model. She has performed parts of *Love Street* with jazz musicians in Toronto.

Susan Perly was born in Toronto, where she lives with her husband, the poet Dennis Lee.